Praise for *Kerka's*

"This sparkling combination of action and magic is bound to enchant."
—*Kirkus Reviews*

"Excellent. . . . The writing is refreshingly well done and weaves together the author's knowledge of art, folklore, and botany to paint a magical world where readers' senses are piqued by the likes of stone fairies, cave anemones, and a queen named Patchouli."
—*SLJ*

"Great for girls who love fairies and magical worlds."
—KidzWorld.com

Praise for *Birdie's Book*

"Bozarth's tale is a beguiling mix of magic, adventure and eco-awareness, and her message of girl-power and positive change will resonate with tween readers."
—*Kirkus Reviews*

"A fun, light read that ought to be a hit with girls who like adventure and magic."
—Books for Kids (blog)

"Bozarth has taken the best aspects of various young adult genres and mixed them together in a fresh and optimistic way."
—Kidsreads.com

The Fairy Godmother Academy

The Fairy Godmother Academy

BOOK 5

Sumi's Book

Jan Bozarth

A YEARLING BOOK

Copyright © 2011 by FGA Media Inc.

All rights reserved. Published in the United States by Yearling, an imprint of Random House Children's Books, a division of Random House, Inc., New York.

Yearling and the jumping horse design are registered trademarks of Random House, Inc.

"A Little Piece of Sky" copyright © 2003 by Blue Arrow Inc.

Visit us on the Web!
randomhouse.com/kids

Educators and librarians, for a variety of teaching tools, visit us at randomhouse.com/teachers

Visit FairyGodmotherAcademy.com

Library of Congress Cataloging-in-Publication Data
Bozarth, Jan.
Sumi's book / Jan Bozarth. — 1st Yearling ed.
p. cm. — (The Fairy Godmother Academy ; bk. 5)
Summary: When Sumi Hara finds her family's magical hand-mirror talisman, she dreams her way to the enchanted land of Aventurine where, as a fairy-godmother-in-training, she discovers her individual power with the help of her handsome guide, Kano.
ISBN 978-0-375-86575-6 (pbk.) — ISBN 978-0-375-96575-3 (lib. bdg.) — ISBN 978-0-375-89605-7 (ebook)
[1. Fairy godmothers—Fiction. 2. Fairies—Fiction. 3. Magic—Fiction. 4. Adventure and adventurers—Fiction. 5. Japanese Americans—Fiction.]
I. Title.
PZ7.B6974Sum 2011 [Fic]—dc22 2010047797

Printed in the United States of America
10 9 8 7 6 5 4 3 2 1

First Yearling Edition 2011

To all the beautiful girls in my life:
Bella, Kailey, Andrea, Cameron,
Marie, Tara, Angela, Lurleen,
Meredith, Dee, Sherry, and Jesyca

Contents

Part One
Discovering the Seams

1

Hidden Treasures

Mystic Moments was the exact opposite of the designer-label clothing boutiques I wanted to check out. The store sold antiques from around the world. I didn't shop at stuffy, old places unless my mother dragged me, which she did—often.

Short and trim with a touch of gray in her straight black shoulder-length hair, Osen Hara is an expert in Asian art and antiquities. She finds artifacts, authenticates them, and displays them in galleries and museums. She can't resist the lure of forgotten relics waiting to be rescued from obscurity. She saw Mystic Moments on her way to an appointment to select Japanese kitchenware for our new apartment. She insisted on taking me along when she went back.

We'd been in New York for three weeks now, and would be on our own until my father arrived from

Japan in a week to start his new job. For now, she just had me.

Even though I didn't share Okasan's affection for worn-out, obsolete junk, I didn't resist. I just lagged behind as we climbed the stone steps so she wouldn't see me roll my eyes.

As we stepped through the heavy wooden doors into the dimly lit store, my mother paused and glanced around with an appreciative smile.

I wrinkled my nose and tried not to sneeze.

The aisles were cluttered with barrels, large objects, and display racks. Baskets full of merchandise sat on wooden counters, and shelves were crammed with books, folded clothes, and knickknacks. Scratchy classical music played softly in the background.

"Isn't this charming, Sumi?" my mother asked. She spoke English fluently—our family had agreed to speak only English during our first year in New York. We were all pretty good at it already thanks to English classes in Japan, but my parents insisted on my being completely fluent as quickly as possible.

"It smells funny, Okasan," I whispered, convinced that the musty odor was laced with toxic mold.

Okasan breathed in deeply. "Leather and lavender with a touch of silver polish," she said.

The elderly woman behind a glass jewelry case looked up. She smiled and raised a silver candlestick. "I just finished cleaning it."

"What an interesting piece." Okasan stepped closer to examine the candlestick.

"It's a fabulous example of a colonial silversmith's work." The woman turned the candlestick upside down and handed it to my mother. "It has a family mark on the bottom."

"Is that the artisan's signature?" Okasan asked.

"No, it signifies ownership," the clerk explained. "Most early American towns didn't have banks. So instead of hiding their money, rich people turned their coins into silver objects. When stolen pieces were recovered, the owner could identify his property by the mark."

"Who owned the candlestick?" Okasan asked.

The clerk sighed. "Unfortunately, that information was lost long ago."

The music stopped, but the scratchy sound continued.

"What's that noise?" I asked.

My mother stiffened slightly.

The woman peered at me over the rim of her glasses, like a disapproving teacher. "That noise is called *Sea Drift* by Delius. It was recorded in 1929."

A few awkward seconds passed before I realized my goof. "The music was fine," I said. "I meant the noise now."

"Oh!" The clerk turned toward a large wooden cabinet with a raised lid. She lifted a brass disk that was connected to a brass arm, and the scratchy sound stopped. When she lowered the disk, the music started over from the beginning.

Okasan added a compliment to help smooth things over. "Your gramophone works remarkably well."

"It was made in 1917. It only plays records that were produced before World War Two." The woman held up a black record with a grooved surface. "The old needle is too thick for the grooves on more recent seventy-eights."

Okasan noticed my perplexed look. "Records that play at seventy-eight revolutions per minute," she explained. "Hi-fis and stereos were introduced in the fifties and sixties. They played forty-fives and thirty-threes."

"Now it's MP3s," the clerk said with a sigh. When the music began to drag, she grabbed a metal handle on the side of the gramophone and turned it. "No electricity or batteries required. You just crank it up."

"But you can't carry that music with you." I palmed the tiny MP3 player in my pocket. I was glad I lived now and not way back then.

"That's quite true," the clerk said.

My mother changed the subject before I insulted the woman again. "Do you know how old the candlestick is, exactly?"

"No, but it dates back to colonial times," the clerk said. "Maybe a little before. It's very old."

"Yes, it is," Okasan said with a reverent nod.

She was being diplomatic. The definition of "very old" is much different in America than it is in Japan. The Pilgrims landed in the New World in 1620, and the United States has only been a country since 1776. Kyoto, the city where I grew up, became the imperial capital of Japan in 794. Combs, pottery, and weapons dating back to 11,000 BC have been found in the Japanese islands. *That's* old.

"It would be an honor to have a genuine piece of this country's history," my mother said. She rolled the silver candlestick in her hands.

I recognized the signs of an impulse purchase. I do the same thing with clothes, and sometimes I really hate the things I buy as soon as I get home. Okasan can't always stop me from making costly mistakes, but I might be able to keep her from making one.

"The stem isn't straight," I said, "and the pattern is kind of off."

"It's handcrafted," the clerk pointed out. "Colonial methods weren't exact."

"The imperfections are what make this piece so precious," Okasan said.

I persisted. "It doesn't match our Japanese furniture."

Okasan gave me a pointed look. "Art does not have to match the decor."

I gave up. Why press an argument I couldn't win?

My mother is the essence of *wabi-sabi*, a perception of life and the world that Japanese culture has embraced for centuries. She sees something beautiful about everything, even if it's very old, very gross, or very ugly. Sometimes I wonder if her love of flaws has anything to do with the crescent-shaped scar on her face. I don't know what I would do if my cheek were scarred like that. I would probably point out the good in imperfections, too. But I've never asked her about the scar. People get insulted really easily about their looks, and I don't want to make her feel bad.

Okasan gave the candlestick back to the clerk. "Will you hold this while we look around?"

"Of course!" The woman smiled and set the piece by a large antique cash register.

My mother began a methodical exploration of the aisles. "If you find anything you like, Sumi, consider it an early birthday present."

"Thanks," I said, but I wasn't hopeful about finding anything. I was turning thirteen in two weeks, and I had my eye on some killer heels that my mom would never have let me wear in Japan. I was hoping that in the next few weeks she would realize that the fashion in New York City was a lot less conservative than back home.

I wandered past wood and metal toys, jars of dried herbs and spices, sewing notions, books, and bins of weird household utensils. A display of old dress patterns caught my eye, but I didn't stop to look. I'd just spotted clothing racks in the back corner of the store where I might be able to discover some vintage designer pieces.

I'm passionate about fashion, and someday I'll be a famous designer. There's no doubt in my mind. I wear the latest styles, and I'm not afraid to make alterations and add my own touches. I've even started a few trends. One day, I wore mismatched kneesocks with a skirt that was part of my old school's uniform. I liked the funky look. Soon all the girls were wearing mismatched kneesocks—it was suddenly lame to match—just because I'd started wearing them.

I'm tall and slim, so I look great in clothes— especially a Japanese kimono, which Okasan and I wear to weddings and other traditional events. We don't do it very often. Kimonos are so complicated, my mother has to hire a professional to help us dress.

Obviously, we wouldn't be wearing kimonos in New York. I needed new pieces for my wardrobe immediately.

I pulled a gray pleated skirt off a

rack and then put it back. It was much too bland for my taste. I didn't know what the students at the Girls' International School of Manhattan usually wore, but it didn't matter. I had already chosen my outfit for the first day: a shocking pink sweater with a black skirt, black tights, and ankle boots. Some kids like to blend into the background until they figure out who's who and what's what in a new school. I like to stand out.

A glint of light reflected off a full-length mirror on the wall, drawing my gaze. I wrinkled my nose at my image. I had worn tailored tan pants and a basic white blouse to please my mother. Even my long, shiny black hair looked plain without a beaded headband or sparkling barrettes, but I didn't let the dull look dampen my mood. I was still pretty with large oval eyes and a flawless complexion.

"Do you need help?" the clerk asked, coming over to stand by me.

"No, thank you. I'm having fun looking." I took a white dress off a rack and gasped. "This is gorgeous!"

"It was hand sewn in the twenties," the woman said.

I touched the fabric with awed amazement. The white silk tulle was heavily embroidered. The short sleeves and knee-length hem were made of knotted lace. With a scooped neck and empire waist, the dress was as perfect for an afternoon in the twenty-first

9

century as it had been almost a hundred years ago.

And it looked like my size!

"Would you like to try it on?" the clerk asked.

"Absolutely!" I grinned as I stepped into the curtained fitting room, then looked out again. "Do you have shoes to go with it? I'm a six."

The woman left and returned with a pair of rose-colored T-strap pumps with a thick three-inch heel. The dress seemed to fit, but I stepped out to look in the full-length mirror. "What do you think?" I asked, but I was just being polite. I didn't care what she thought. I'm very particular about everything I wear. If I don't like what I see, I don't waste my time.

"That dress was made for you," the clerk said.

I twirled in front of the mirror and then stopped to shift my weight from one side to the other with a hand on my hip. This dress might be perfect for my profile picture. I turned my back to the glass, twisted, and glanced over my shoulder to the left and the right. The dress flowed with my movements beautifully.

"It's perfect," the saleswoman added.

"Almost," I said. "If I had a beaded bag, *then* it would be perfect."

"You'll find bags and accessories over there." She pointed toward shelves and a table of bins.

I changed back into my boring shopping outfit,

gave the new outfit to the clerk, and hurried toward the shelves.

Several hats were on display. Some sat at perky angles on faceless plastic heads. All the price tags included a date. A few of the styles were too clunky for my small frame, and most of the colors were too gaudy or drab.

I picked up a bell-shaped cloche from the mid-twenties. The hat and narrow brim were covered in eggshell-white lace. The cloth flowers attached to one side had faded to a pretty shade of pink. It wasn't too big or too snug and looked fantastic on my black hair. I wouldn't wear it with the old-fashioned dress—that would be too matchy-matchy—but it would look great with jeans and a simple white top.

I set the cloche aside to look at bags, which didn't have a special place on the shelves or in the bins. Everything was jumbled together, and I had to sort through scarves, combs, brushes, coin purses, brooches, and dozens of other items. Taking care not to damage anything, I tackled the search with an enthusiasm that reminded me of Okasan when she unpacks artifacts from an archaeological dig.

There weren't any beaded bags in the first bin, but

I found a blue rhinestone butterfly brooch. I would have adored it when I was six.

When I moved the top layer of scarves and handkerchiefs in the second bin, I finally found a scalloped beaded evening bag, but its chain strap was buried under a wooden box. Being careful not to snag the chain on anything, I lifted the box. It was heavier than I expected. Dust and grime had settled into the crevices of the bird, flower, and leaf design carved into the wood. The lid was held in place by tarnished metal hinges and a matching clasp. I opened the box, expecting to find small trays and compartments, but was surprised.

The bottom was lined with padded silk, which, over time, had formfitted around a brass hand mirror. The embossed leafy vines on the handle and the elegant bird, flower, and leaf design on the back matched the carving on the box. However, the mirror glass was missing, making it interesting but completely useless. I put the mirror back in its silk nest and closed the lid.

But despite my loathing for dirty, broken old things, something about the box and hand mirror kept me from putting them back in the bin. I've learned a lot about ancient Asian artifacts from my mother. I was almost certain that the box and hand mirror were very old by Japanese standards, not American. The mirror made me think of Amaterasu, the Japanese Shinto sun goddess. Her story had been my childhood favorite, and Okasan had never tired of telling the myth over and over again.

Okasan used to say that Amaterasu was so beautiful and bright, her father made her the ruler of the heavens. This made her brother, Susanoo, the storm god, very angry. Susanoo battered the earth with hard rains and deafening thunder that drove his shining sister into a cave. Fearing her brother's wrath, Amaterasu blocked the entrance of the cave with a giant rock and sealed herself inside.

Without light to ward them off, the monsters of the dark roamed freely over the world. The other gods tried everything to lure Amaterasu out of hiding. Nothing worked until Amenouzume, the goddess of joy and celebration, came up with a plan.

Amenouzume laughed while she hung a mirror from a tree branch near the entrance to Amaterasu's cave. Drawn by the sound of her joyful mischief, the other gods gathered around. When Amenouzume began to dance, they thought it was so funny they *all* began to laugh.

The laughter caught Amaterasu's attention. Curious about the fuss, she moved the rock to peek out of the cave. When she saw her brilliant reflection in the mirror hanging from the tree, she stepped outside to look closer.

The gods quickly sealed the cave entrance with a magic rope so she couldn't get back in. Then they begged her to roll back the darkness. Amaterasu listened to the pleas and returned to the heavens to shine her light on the world. In her Shinto temple on the island of Honshu, Amaterasu's divine being is represented by a mirror.

"Did you find something you like?" my mother asked, breaking me out of my reverie.

"Yes, and something you might like, too." I held out the carved box.

"You found it!" Okasan gasped with delight, and her hands trembled as she took the box.

My mother is usually really reserved, even when she's happy. I couldn't figure out why she was so excited, unless she thought I'd found some long-lost relic. When she purchased the box along with my dress and accessories, I figured it would end up in a museum display. I didn't know until we left the shop that she had bought it for me.

"Shouldn't something like this be in a museum, where everyone can appreciate it?" I asked, trying to be diplomatic. I couldn't picture where I would stick the box in my room.

Okasan shook her head. "This mirror has special meaning for you."

I frowned in confusion. Maybe the box and the mirror weren't valuable ancient artifacts after all. Maybe my mother just thought I had finally seen beauty in pieces of old junk. The mirror had made me remember one of my favorite stories, but it really didn't reflect my style. It didn't reflect anything. The glass was gone.

But Okasan was so happy that I just smiled. It would be ungracious to refuse the gift, but I hoped she wouldn't notice if I kept the grimy old box in a drawer.

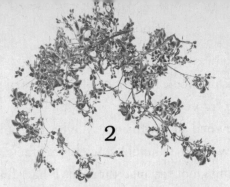

2

Fairy Tales and Tea

We flagged a taxi on the corner and got in before it started to rain. As we drove off, I realized Okasan hadn't even opened the box before she bought it.

"There's a hand mirror inside the box," I said. "But the glass is missing."

"I know," Okasan said.

"How could you know?" I asked, puzzled. "You didn't look at it."

"I'll explain when we get home." Okasan folded her hands around the old box in her lap, as though protecting a precious treasure.

I don't usually waste time or energy trying to pry secrets out of people—I always find stuff out eventually. But my mother's mysterious answers were too odd to ignore. I pestered her with questions, which she refused to answer.

"I'll tell you everything you need to know, Sumi," Okasan said, "but not in the back of a taxi."

I held my tongue as we exited the cab with our bags, walked through the lobby of our building, and rode the elevator up to the fifteenth floor. The instant we entered our apartment, my patience broke.

"Are we going to talk about the box now?" I asked as I kicked off my shoes onto a mat by the door.

"Yes," Okasan said. "I'll make tea."

I hesitated before I turned down the hall. "What should I wear?" I wanted to change into comfy shorts and a tank top, but that wouldn't be appropriate for a tea ceremony.

The Japanese people have many ancient cultural customs. I respect all of them, but the Way of the Tea is my favorite.

The Japanese tea ceremony is a form of *wabi* that honors age, imperfection, and the unadorned. The preparation and serving of green tea are precise, and the formal ritual in the presence of guests can last for hours. My mother performs the tea ceremony only on very special occasions. She was acting so weird about the box, I didn't know if today was one of those occasions.

"Put on something comfortable," Okasan said. "I'll make tea in the kitchen and bring it out."

Okasan set the box on the tea table and cradled the silver candlestick as she studied the living room. I could tell she was looking for exactly the right spot.

My mother had chosen the furniture and accents in our new apartment with great care, and everything was placed just so. The tea table sat in the wide space between two sand-colored couches. Two matching side tables, one at opposite ends of each couch, and a *mizuya* were the only other furniture. With many drawers and cabinets, the wooden *mizuya* resembled an entertainment center without the TV. Books, the tea ceremony cups and implements, and a few board games were stored inside it.

That's right. I said no TV. My parents think TV will rot my brain, which means I have to stream all my shows online. How else can I stay on top of the hottest fashions? I just have to remember to keep the volume really low.

Okasan placed the colonial candlestick on a side table by two small books of Japanese poems. The gleaming silver complemented the leather-bound paper and blended with the minimal, Asian-chic decor.

Only the carved box on the table stood out.

I headed down the hall to my bedroom. Hanging out at Mystic Moments with my mother, surrounded by antiques, had drained me. The vibrant colors in my room were the shot of energy that I needed.

The headboard, computer desk, dresser, storage chest, and nightstand were simple in design and made of light oak. Everything else—the curtains, pillows, bedspread, blankets, and wallpaper borders—was shades of bright green with pale yellow and pinks. My cloth-covered desk chair was green with large white, pink, and yellow polka dots.

I dropped my shopping bags on the bed and turned to hang my new dress in the closet. Then I quickly changed out of the shopping-with-Okasan outfit and into my favorite comfy purple shorts and a soft vintage tee of a band I'd never heard of but loved because it had worn thin with age.

The neon-green numbers on my digital alarm clock read 4:38. It was late afternoon in New York and not quite dawn the next day in Kyoto. The time difference made real-time communication difficult. My friends were having breakfast while I was having dinner, and they were in school while I was asleep.

I checked my email anyway.

Hisako had written me three times in just a few hours!

I glanced at the photo of Hisako, Eiko, and me on the desk beside my laptop. We were all smiling. The picture had been taken right before we lost a volleyball game. I almost never lose anything, so I definitely didn't keep the photo to remember the game, but we all looked so fantastic, it was hard not to frame it. I was glad I did, since it cheered me up to see my friends, even if I couldn't see them in person.

The tea water hadn't had time to boil, so I sat down to read Hisako's emails.

Sumi!
There's a totally gorgeous new boy at school. His name is Akiyo. I think he likes me! He's talked to me every day this week. When can you IM? MISS YOU!!!
Hisako xx

That was news! I'm always getting texts and calls from boys who like me. They're all nice, but they're not boyfriend material. I'm waiting for someone who's really special.

Eiko is cute and funny, so boys like her, too. She changes boyfriends like I change clothes.

Hisako is the shy one in our group. She's a bit of a bookworm and can be very proper. She hardly ever talks to boys. I hoped she wasn't misreading Akiyo's attention.

I crossed my fingers and opened the second email.

Sumi,
Why haven't you written back? I have to go to sleep soon. I hate that you're so far away. I wish you were

here so I could talk to you anytime!
Hisako

I wanted to shout, "I have things to do! I'm getting settled in a new country!" There was no point, of course. Hisako was half a world away, and she can't take a hint anyway. I opened her last email.

Are you mad at me?
Hisako

I sighed. Hisako worries about everything. It's annoying, and I didn't want to keep my mother waiting. But Hisako would worry all day if I didn't write back, so I sent a quick reply.

Hisako!
I'm not mad. I'm busy. Okasan took me shopping—
at an antique store! Sigh. ;) I'll ttyl, before I go to
sleep. Can you IM at lunch?
Sumi

Feeling good about how I'd handled Hisako's drama, I returned to the living room just as Okasan knelt to set a tray on the tea table. I sat on a pillow and waited while she poured green tea into blue tea bowls. They don't have handles like teacups, but the

pottery is thick so they don't get too hot to touch.

I took a sip and smiled. Okasan had steeped it just long enough. The taste was mildly sweet and not at all bitter. I don't understand why tea never fails to relax me, but it does.

"And a special treat." Okasan set a small plate in front of me and removed the white napkin.

"Almond berry cakes!" I took a plump blueberry off one of the chocolate cake squares and popped it my mouth.

Okasan lifted her tea bowl and sat back on her heels. "Now we can talk about the hand mirror."

I finished chewing and swallowed. "What about the box?"

"It's what's inside the box that counts." Okasan said.

"But the hand mirror is broken," I said.

"The hand mirror is the ancient talisman of the Yugen Lineage of fairy godmothers." Okasan held my gaze. "It appears when a girl is ready to begin her training in Aventurine."

Okasan's stories about young girls on dangerous quests in a fantastic fairy world had thrilled me when I was young. I was much too old for fairy tales now.

"You're almost thirteen, Sumi," Okasan went on.

Exactly, I thought.

"It's your turn to go." My mother's expression was serious, and she spoke without a hint of humor. "Soon."

I was so stunned I couldn't think of what to say. I took a long sip of tea to cover my expression of disbelief.

"I know it's a shock," Okasan continued, "but you must be prepared for what lies ahead."

"You mean a mission?" I hoped I didn't sound as skeptical as I felt. The girls in her stories tamed giant serpents with songs, used dancing sticks to fly, and rode avalanches on magical sleds!

"Yes," Okasan said. "Every fairy godmother in the Yugen Lineage must repair the mirror. You'll be sent on a quest to find the five missing shards."

"What kind of a quest?" I asked.

"I do not know," Okasan said.

"Didn't you go on one?" I was sure I had found a hole in her story.

"Yes, but the mission is different for every girl." Okasan poured more tea into my bowl.

The idea that all my female ancestors had been fairy godmothers was just too preposterous. However, my mother was clearly trying hard to make me believe it. Eventually, I'd figure out why. I'd just have to humor her until I did.

Okasan opened the carved box, removed the hand mirror, and passed it to me. "Most fairy godmother lineage talismans stay with the family."

"Then why was the Yugen mirror at Mystic Moments?" I peered into the glass that wasn't there. The polished brass inside the frame gleamed but didn't reflect anything.

"Once the mission is completed, the mirror disappears and a crescent scar on the girl takes its place." Okasan gently touched the curved mark on her cheek.

I gasped. I had never had a blemish, not even a freckle.

Okasan didn't scold me for being vain. She tried to comfort me with an explanation. "The scar means I successfully completed my quest, Sumi. And that allowed me to continue training to become a fairy godmother. I was happy to get mine."

Despite how unbelievable it all sounded, I had to ask, "What kind of fairy godmother stuff do you do?"

"I find beauty in the world," she said.

My mother finds old junk that she thinks is beautiful. I rarely agree with what she finds beautiful, but I would never say so.

Okasan mistook my silence for worry. "You're a smart, resourceful girl. I'm sure you'll succeed in Aventurine, too."

I wasn't worried about failing. I just wasn't sure I wanted to succeed if I'd be scarred for life! Of course, that would only be a problem if Okasan's stories were true.

Fairy godmothers and Aventurine couldn't possibly be real, could they?

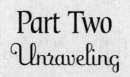

Part Two
Unraveling

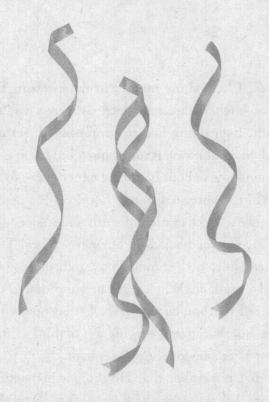

3

Shifting Dreams

After tea, I helped my mother in the kitchen. Three boxes of kitchenware had been delivered while we were out. Everything had to be unpacked, set up or washed, and put away. It took hours, but Okasan told me funny stories about her latest experiences in New York. Things were so different here!

We ate a light dinner of miso soup, rice, and a cucumber-seaweed salad on our new dishes. Then I went straight to bed, stopping only to brush my teeth and wash my face. When I got to my room, Okasan had placed the box on my desk. I tried not to think about it, but that was like trying not to think about an elephant after someone says "elephant."

I didn't remember that Hisako was expecting to chat until I was under the covers. My clean sheets were cool and comfortable, and I was too tired to get up. Besides, my mother's sanity was more important than my friend's love life.

Okasan hadn't mentioned the fairy world again, but she seemed to believe in it. I wasn't sure which was more unsettling: if my mother were delusional, or if the stories were true! Now I wished I had pressed for details about her mission. What could my down-to-earth mother have accomplished in a magical world?

I fell asleep imagining a young Osen Hara battling monsters in an Aventurine garden.

I woke up wondering why my brand-new mattress was soft and squishy. And why the scent of dried herbs and salt air tickled my nose. When I opened my eyes, I realized I was still dreaming.

A fairy stood on a rock pedestal a few feet away. Hints of green, red, and blue glittered in her silver wings. No jewelry, flowers, or shells broke the sleek lines of her long silver hair and shimmering silver gown. Although she didn't have fins or a tail, she reminded me of a beautiful silvery fish.

"Who are you?" I asked in a voice raspy with sleep.

"I am Queen Kumari," the fairy answered. Her voice echoed like crystal chimes in a great hall.

"Of course." I smiled and nodded knowingly.

Most Japanese children are familiar with our many gods and goddesses. Apparently, I had dreamed up my own version of the Shinto water goddess, Ame-No-Mi-Kumari, a warrior who can control water and summon lightning bolts.

My silver Kumari was prettier and much nicer, I decided.

"Queen Patchouli of the Willowood Fairies sent me to help you begin your mission," Queen Kumari said.

"Okay." I yawned and stretched. My hand hit something much harder than my oak headboard. I sat up with a jolt.

I was not in my yellow, green, and pink bedroom in New York City. I was sitting on a nest of sea grasses in a large cavern. It was softly lit by thousands of sparkling crystals in the ceiling. Except for the grass bed and the fairy's rock pedestal, the cave was empty.

It all felt so real. I suddenly began to doubt that I was still asleep! Plus, I never would've imagined myself in such a plain setting.

"All fairy-godmothers-in-training must record their life's dream when they enter Aventurine the first time," Queen Kumari said.

"I don't remember entering Aventurine," I said.

"You dreamed your way in," the fairy explained.

"How long will I be here?"

"Only one night will pass where you came from," the fairy queen said, "but you are living in Aventurine time now. How long you remain here depends on how long it takes to complete your mission."

And my reward for completing the mission was an ugly scar.

"What happens if I don't complete my mission?" I asked.

"You'll be banned from Aventurine." Queen Kumari looked at me with solemn blue eyes. "And your descendants, too, perhaps."

"That's not fair." This fairy queen was starting to tick me off. Who was she to kick people out?

"Then do not fail." The fairy queen's majestic wings opened and closed, lifting her up and carrying her to the pedestal. A large leather-bound book appeared on the pedestal, and a spongy stool sprang up beside it. "Sit here, Sumi."

My feet were bare, since I was still wearing what I'd worn to bed. I didn't want to step on sharp pebbles or slip on slime, but making excuses didn't seem smart. I wanted to see what happened next. I held my breath and put my feet down.

The rock floor was smooth and hard. Nothing gross was growing on it. I didn't have to hold my arms to ward off chills, either. The air was warm. The sea sponge stool was dry and stiff, and I didn't sink when I sat down. The porous surface just felt a little scratchy on my bare legs.

"What should I do?" I asked.

"Write what you most want from life in *The Book of Dreams*," Queen Kumari said.

I flinched with surprise when the large book suddenly opened to a blank page. I started to ask for a pen, then noticed a shell with a silver lid and a feather quill beside the book. The shell was full of shimmery purple ink. If only my gel pens came in that shimmery color.

This part will be easy, I thought. I had known what I wanted to do since I was four! I dipped the quill pen in the ink and wrote:

I want to be a famous model and fashion designer.

Convinced I was off to a great start, I smiled with satisfaction.

Then all my words vanished!

"What happened?" I stared at the blank page. "Is this invisible ink?"

"No," Queen Kumari said. "Apparently, your dream wasn't acceptable."

"But it's *my* dream!" I protested. "I can't change it. Then it won't be mine."

"You can't begin your quest until your dream is recorded *and* accepted." The fairy tapped her chin. "It might help to read your mother's dream."

I didn't see how, but I was willing to try anything. I hated that a stupid book had rejected my dream.

"I'd be honored to read it," I said.

The book opened to a page written in my mother's graceful hand. Pictures of delicate bonsai trees and red-lace maples filled the four corners. The edges were adorned with lilies, orchids, and sago palms, mixed with primitive tools, pottery, and other artifacts. When I looked closely, I noticed that the pots were cracked and chipped, the tools were bent or rusted, and some of the flowers and plants had torn petals and wilted leaves.

The illustrations perfectly represented my mother and her words:

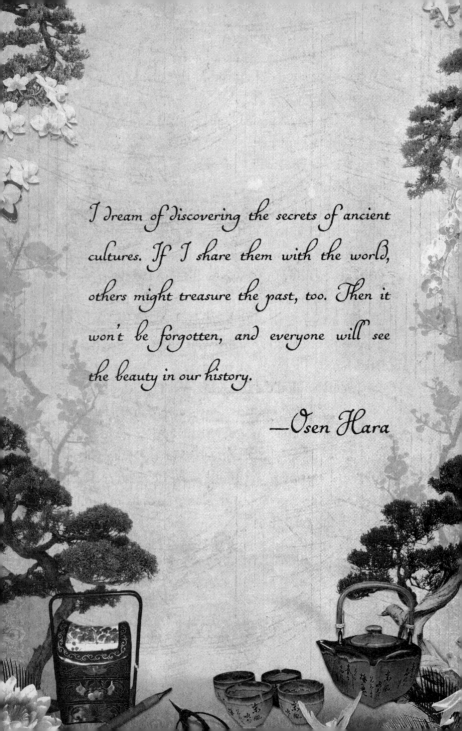

I dream of discovering the secrets of ancient cultures. If I share them with the world, others might treasure the past, too. Then it won't be forgotten, and everyone will see the beauty in our history.

—Osen Hara

The words made me shiver—not with cold, but with awe. My mother's displays of ancient art and artifacts gave people a glimpse of beauty from the past. Her dream had come true.

The book flipped back to my blank page.

"Are you ready?" Queen Kumari asked.

I nodded. My mother's dream had been focused on helping others. My dream did, too. I just had to use the right words. I dipped the pen in ink again and wrote:

I want to design clothes that make girls look fantastic!

My delighted grin faded along with the ink.

The words were gone again!

"What's wrong with that dream?" I folded my arms and exhaled with frustration. "Girls love clothes that look great."

"Why?" Queen Kumari asked.

I shrugged. The answer was so obvious. "Because nice clothes make them . . . Oh!" Hoping the obvious answer was the key, I picked up the pen again.

I want to design clothes that make girls feel good inside and out. Clothes that are so beautiful, they show off the beauty and confidence of the girl wearing them.

—Sumi Hara

I shut my eyes, took a deep breath, and opened them slowly.

My words were still on the page!

I watched as pictures of jeweled Japanese hair sticks, kimono bows, sewing needles and colored threads, ribbons, buttons, cherry blossoms, and lilies filled up the empty space on the page.

"It's beautiful." As I reached out to touch the page, *The Book of Dreams* slammed closed. The book, quill pen, and ink shell blinked out. The fairy queen continued to hover.

"What did Okasan do next?" I asked.

"Like most girls, she chose appropriate clothing from the Willowood Fairy wardrobe," Queen Kumari said. "However—"

"Clothes!" I exclaimed, cutting her off. I didn't mean to be rude, but a fairy wardrobe was just too exciting. I jumped up. "Can I see?"

Queen Kumari frowned, as though she were undecided.

I clasped my hands and begged, "Please!"

"As you wish," the fairy said, flicking her wrist.

The stone pedestal and sponge stool sank into the rock floor, and a wide wooden panel rose up. A painting of two beautiful geishas dressed in traditional kimonos decorated the front of the panel. One held a samisen, a three-stringed Japanese instrument. The other had a drum called a *ko-tsuzumi.* It was narrow in the middle with drum skins stretched over rings at both ends and tied together with thick strings. The wooden panel suddenly expanded into a large chest with two doors on the top. The bottom had many drawers with brass handles, like a *mizuya.*

The transformation happened quickly, but I was still dancing with impatience. When it seemed like the process was finished, I glanced at Queen Kumari. "Can I look now?" I asked.

The fairy nodded, and I opened the doors. The first thing I saw was the broken Yugen mirror lying on a shelf. I ignored it to check out the fabulous clothes draped on hangers and pegs.

The fabrics and materials were as varied as the styles: gossamer chiffon and satiny silk dresses and skirts; leather leggings; homespun tunics; fleece-lined jackets; cargo-type pants and snug capris; ruffled tops; blouses with sweeping, dramatic sleeves; and luxurious knit sweaters.

There were so many choices, I didn't know where to begin. I was in absolute heaven.

Eventually, my eye was drawn to a gray-blue dress draped in an almost Grecian style. I pressed the soft, delicate fabric against my cheek.

"I love this," I said, "but I'm not sure what shoes to wear with it."

"Decide quickly, please," the fairy queen said. "It doesn't matter what you wear."

I laughed. "It *always* matters what I wear."

Unlike the bins at Mystic Moments, each drawer in the fairy *mizuya* was devoted to a particular item. I found a darling pair of lace-up leather sandals among the boots and slippers in the shoes drawer. In case Aventurine was colder outside the cave, I also picked out a silvery silk scarf that would look amazing with the gray-blue dress.

I quickly changed into the dress and laced up the sandals. Then I found a drawer of bracelets and slipped on a bunch of beautiful beaded ones. The beads clicked in a satisfying way when I moved. I wondered if I looked as magical as I felt.

I wound the scarf around my neck and turned to Queen Kumari. The fairy queen's serene face showed no signs of impatience.

"Do you have a mirror?" I asked.

Queen Kumari glided across the floor. She reached into the wardrobe and picked up the Yugen hand mirror. Before I could remind her that the mirror had no glass, the wardrobe flattened and sank back into the floor.

"This is the only mirror you'll need." The fairy queen handed it to me. "It's called Takara."

"Uh-huh." *Takara* means "treasure" in Japanese.

I stared at the gleaming brass where the mirror glass should have been, but I couldn't see my reflection.

"Listen, Sumi," Queen Kumari said sharply. "Every word I say will be of vital importance on your journey."

"Yes, I'm sorry." My cheeks burned with embarrassment. I held the hand mirror behind my back and gave her my full attention.

"You must find the five shards of Takara's missing glass," the fairy continued. "As you secure each shard, it will automatically be attracted to its proper place in the mirror frame."

"How am I supposed to find five little pieces of glass?" I knew from Okasan's stories that the fairy world was full of strange places and dangerous creatures. "Aventurine is too big."

"Your ancestors did it," Queen Kumari said. "Surely you're as intelligent and capable as they were."

I couldn't disagree without looking really stupid.

"There is one hint I can give you," the fairy added. "The last shard lies beneath Bristolmeir, at the bottom of the sea."

I blinked. I was a good swimmer, but I couldn't

breathe underwater. Then I remembered my mother's stories. The girls were always given things that helped them accomplish their tasks. Did Queen Kumari have a big spiral shell that would magically turn into scuba gear?

As if on cue, Queen Kumari said, "Queen Patchouli has three gifts for you."

"What are they?" I asked eagerly.

"The words 'Takara's truth,'" the fairy said. "They will make the Yugen mirror disappear and reappear."

That wasn't as exotic or exciting as I had imagined, but at least I wouldn't have to carry the mirror the whole time. I could make it go away until I needed it.

"What else?" I asked, hoping for something better.

Queen Kumari smiled and swept her arm across the space where the wardrobe had been. The stone pedestal emerged again. This time a huge layer cake with pink and yellow icing flowers and green jelly leaves sat on top of it.

"That looks delicious," I said. "Will Queen Patchouli be insulted if I can't eat it all?"

"No." The fairy queen laughed. "One piece will be more than enough."

"Oh, good." I smiled and nodded. "Do you want a piece?"

"No, thank you," Queen Kumari said. "But your third gift might like cake."

What kind of Aventurine gift had a sweet tooth?

"Come here, Kano," she said.

I turned and gasped.

My third gift was the most gorgeous boy I had ever seen.

4

Piece of Cake

Kano bowed his head toward Queen Kumari. "I am here as requested."

"Queen Patchouli has sent Kano to be your guide," Queen Kumari told me. "He knows the ways of Aventurine. It would be wise to listen to him."

Before I could thank her, the fairy queen faded into the wall. Just faded away! I shrugged it off. Weird things probably happened all the time in magical places, and I was more interested in my gifts, especially my guide.

Kano was dressed in a blue tunic belted over a white shirt and gray leggings. The tops of his black boots were turned over like a pirate's, but he didn't wear a gold hoop in his ear or a skull-and-crossbones hat on his handsome head. With a mop of curly brown hair, large green eyes, and a slightly lopsided grin, he looked exactly like the boy of my dreams.

"Hello, Sumi," Kano said. His voice sounded like melted caramel, smooth and warm.

I was too captivated to talk.

"Is something wrong?" Kano asked.

"You're so—so beautiful," I stammered, then silently scolded myself for acting like a lovesick groupie. Kano wasn't a rock star. I usually didn't have any trouble flirting with boys, and then I'd gone and called this one *beautiful*. *He must think I'm really lame,* I thought.

Kano shrugged. "What you think doesn't make it so."

I frowned. How rude! Was he seriously mocking me? I couldn't tell. Feeling oddly flustered, I tried to prove my point. "You have to know you're good-looking. Anyone would agree with me."

"Perhaps," Kano said, "but a scarlet swamp bat would be repulsed by my appearance."

"Um, okay. But I'm not a bat." I held up the broken mirror. "When this mirror is fixed, you'll see what you look like."

Kano looked into the empty brass frame. "What I see doesn't change the truth of what I said."

Baffled and a bit perturbed, I glanced at the mirror. I saw Kano's distorted image in the polished brass. I turned the empty frame to face me. "That's strange."

"You are a little strange," Kano said.

"Not me!" I sounded more upset than I intended. I didn't want him to think his opinion mattered to me—even though it did. "I meant that your face is reflected in the brass, and mine isn't."

"That is curious," Kano said.

"And troubling." I looked into the mirror from different angles, but it didn't make a difference. My face wasn't reflected back at all.

I caught Kano watching me. His mesmerizing eyes were narrowed with concern.

"Queen Kumari said you know how things work in Aventurine. Why is this happening?" I asked anxiously.

"I have an idea," Kano said.

I waited, feeling more and more awkward as the seconds ticked away. When he didn't continue, I vowed to make my next imaginary boy a lot less infuriating.

"What is it?" I asked with a huff of impatience. I flicked my hair over my shoulder in what I hoped was an imperious way.

"Are you sure you want to know?" Kano asked with a hint of superiority.

Was he teasing? Again, I couldn't tell, so I matched his annoying attitude. "Of course I want to know, but if you don't want to tell me—"

"Sometimes the truth can be hard to take," Kano said.

"I can take anything you dish out," I shot back.

"We'll see." Kano looked me in the eye. "Takara reflects truth. Are you dishonest?"

"No!" I snapped. "I'm not a liar or a cheater."

Kano just looked at me, as though my protest were proof.

"Then perhaps you can't see yourself because there's nothing there to see." A smile played at the corner of Kano's mouth, and there was a distinct twinkle in his eye.

He had to be teasing! I was mad at myself for not realizing it sooner, but teasing was something I knew how to handle.

"That's not nice." I pouted playfully. My parents, my friends, and every boy I've ever met can't stand to see me sad. "Why are you being so mean?"

"I wasn't joking or being mean, Sumi," Kano said. "If Takara doesn't see you, there's something wrong with you."

"What?" The comment caught me off guard, and I reacted with surprised anger. "There's *nothing* wrong with me."

"Then why doesn't Takara see you?" Kano asked calmly.

I tried to think of a stinging comeback, but

everything that came to mind seemed childish. I wasn't sure if Kano was teasing me because that's what boys do or if he just said exactly what he thought. Either way, it hurt my feelings.

And *that* bothered me more than being teased.

I couldn't go on a mission or a quest or whatever with someone who thought I was defective!

Maybe I was testing myself! So I didn't say or do the wrong thing when I finally met the *real* boy of my dreams. Kano might be harder to win over, but I didn't back down from the challenge. I changed tactics.

"Would you like some cake, Kano?" I momentarily imagined myself smushing a piece in his face.

"I'd love some!" Kano grinned.

A wide knife, forks, napkins, and seashell plates were neatly laid out on the pedestal beside the cake. I set down the hand mirror and picked up the knife. Kano leaned in to peer over my shoulder. He smelled clean and fresh, like ocean air and soap.

"Can I have a piece with a sugar flower?" Kano asked. "And one of those leaves?"

"Sure!" I cut a huge piece with three flowers and a cluster of leaves and slid the cake knife underneath it. I had to admit, it was kind of cute how excited he was about the cake. I was forced to use my fingers to keep the big wedge from falling as I moved it onto a plate. "Sorry about the fingers."

"That's okay. I don't mind." Kano took the plate, but he didn't use a fork. He picked up the cake with his hand and took a huge bite. Icing smeared all around his mouth.

"That's disgusting!" I made a sick face. I couldn't help it. Everyone has good manners in Japan. I handed him a napkin.

"It's just cake." Kano shook his head, as though I were being unreasonable, but he wiped the icing off his face. "You are such a girl!"

"You are *so* right!" I smiled so he wouldn't think I was mad. "Girls don't smush their food into their mouths!" I ignored the thought that I had just imagined smushing cake into his face.

"They would if they tasted this cake." Kano took another bite and sighed. "It's really good. You should try it."

I cut myself a smaller piece. I wanted to try this fairy cake, but I didn't want to eat it with my hands. I used a fork and took a dainty bite. A thousand tiny bursts of flavor exploded in my mouth: strawberries and honey laced with vanilla custard and sprinkled with cinnamon and nutmeg.

"This is the best cake I've ever had!" I took another, larger bite.

"Me too," Kano said. "May I have another piece?"

My mouth was full, so I just nodded. I closed my eyes and chewed slowly, savoring the sweet, liquid fire that trickled down my throat and seeped into every cell. My skin felt warm, and my fingers and toes tingled with fizzy bubbles. I had never eaten anything as delicious. The taste and sensations were so vivid and unique, I couldn't possibly have imagined them.

I wasn't dreaming.

I was awake, in Aventurine, and living in fairy time just as Queen Kumari had tried to tell me. I had thought that I had accepted that this was real, but eating fairy food had finally, truly convinced me.

My hands went limp, and my plate and fork clattered on the floor. I stared at Kano. "You're real."

"So are you!" Kano squatted down to pick up my plate and then set both of our plates on the pedestal.

I glanced around, wondering for the first time why I had landed in a cave and not in the land of the Willowood Fairies that my mother had always described. The whole concept of Aventurine would be easier to accept if I were in a green meadow with flowers and fruit trees, bubbling brooks and birds, and fairies serving a scrumptious picnic. I felt like I was being punished with this dreary cave, but I clamped my lips together and didn't complain. I didn't want to make my situation worse. Besides, there were good things about it. I loved my new fairy clothes, and the cake was amazing. I just wasn't wild about my hot guide.

"Sorry, this all just suddenly felt real," I said. Then I blurted out, "Why don't you like me, Kano?"

"Who said I didn't like you?" Kano asked.

"You did!" I exclaimed. "You haven't said one nice thing about me, and I even gave you two pieces of cake!"

"Did you offer me cake because you thought I was hungry?" Kano asked. I hesitated, so he answered the question for me. "No. Or because you thought I might enjoy it?"

"Yes, I thought you might like it," I said.

"Maybe. Maybe not. I think it was really just a bribe to make me like you."

"Did it work?" I looked up into his eyes and nervously twiddled my scarf.

"A little." Kano's mischievous smile lit up the gloomy cave.

I smiled. Finding five small shards of glass was a daunting task. It would be unbearable if Kano and I couldn't get along.

"Would you like some more?" I asked.

"No, thank you." Kano rubbed his flat stomach. "I'm full."

The pedestal collapsed into the floor. The rest of my cake vanished with it, but the hand mirror was left behind on the floor.

"Are you ready to begin?" asked Kano.

"Yes," I said. Now that I knew that Aventurine and my fairy godmother heritage were real, I had to do my best to succeed. I picked up Takara and tried not to think about Okasan's crescent-shaped scar. "Let's go look for mirror shards."

As I spoke, I remembered that Queen Kumari had faded out of the cave. I glanced around, assuming that an exit would magically appear, but the ceiling continued to glitter with an unbroken blanket of crystals and the walls remained solid.

"How did you get in here?" I asked.

"Queen Patchouli's magic transported me," Kano explained.

"Is she going to transport us out?" I asked.

"No, we're on our own." Kano grinned with boyish enthusiasm. "It'll be fun. Just follow me, and do what I do."

I didn't understand, but I remembered Queen Kumari's advice. Kano knew what he was doing, and I had to trust him. I gripped Takara, braced myself, and then screamed.

Kano had turned into a snake!

Horrified, I jumped back.

The yellowish-green serpent with a black squiggle on its back raised its broad head. "Ready?" the snake asked in Kano's voice, and looked at me with Kano's very human eyes.

I was still in shock, but it was too late to back out. The tingling in my fingers and toes became an intense buzzing that spread through my veins like molten metal. My body felt as though every muscle had fallen asleep, the way my foot does when I sit on it too long. Then my bones cracked, and I screamed again.

"Relaxxxx," Kano said. "Morphing issss pain-lesssss."

"Sheasy fo' 'ou t'shay!" I couldn't talk. My teeth and tongue were changing shape in my mouth.

"Don't fight it, Ssssumi. Your body will automatically copy whatever form I take."

That didn't make me feel better. I was turning into a snake, and there was nothing I could do about it. Plus, I looked completely ridiculous, while Kano's shift from boy to reptile had been quick.

I had no conscious control, but my body seemed to know what it was doing. Slowly and awkwardly, I began to transform. My head flattened, and my shoulders shriveled. Takara fell on the hard floor when I lost my hands.

"Careful!" Kano slithered over to the heirloom.

"It didn't break," I said. "There'ssss no glasssss."

My face had completed the transition into the head of an ugly snake. I assumed I had human eyes and looked just as repulsive as Kano. But at least I could talk again.

"Sssstill, you shouldn't be sssso carelesssss with your family'ssss mosssst treassssured possssssessss-sion," Kano said. His eyes narrowed with disapproval.

"You should have warned me I wouldn't have fingerssss to hold it," I hissed, and flicked my forked tongue at him.

"Okay, you've got a point," Kano admitted. "But from now on, just ussssse the magic phrassssse Queen Patchouli gave you."

I had forgotten about the fairy queen's first gift, but I hadn't forgotten the words. When I said "Takara'ssss truth," the hand mirror disappeared in a flash of golden light.

Finally, I felt that the shift was complete. I curled into a coil and drew back as though to strike, testing my new form. I didn't have to concentrate on what I was doing; the movements came naturally. I still had the thoughts and emotions of Sumi Hara the girl, but physically I was a snake.

And I was mad.

There were *billions* of creatures in the waking

world and probably in Aventurine, too. I suspected that Kano had picked the horrid reptile because he knew I would hate it.

"Why did you turn ussss into ssssnakessss?" I asked.

"It'ssss the only form that can leave the cavern without fairy help," Kano said.

That made sense, I guess. I felt bad for thinking the worst about Kano's motives and was glad that snakes couldn't blush.

I uncoiled and moved toward him. By flexing my body from one side to the other, I created a wave motion that pushed me across the uneven rock floor.

"When did I become a shape-shifter?" I asked.

"You've alwaysss been one," Kano said. "Everyone in the Yugen Lineage issss a shape-shifter."

"But I can't shape-shift at home," I said. Changing clothes and hairstyles probably didn't count.

"You've alwaysss had the power; you jusssst didn't know how to usssse it. The cake gave you the nudge you needed," Kano said. "And I provided the pattern."

I couldn't frown, so I twitched the end of my tail. "Doessss that mean I'll turn into whatever nassssty creature you chooosssse?"

"Yessss, until the cake wearssss off and you learn to control the ability," Kano said. "You'll be ssssafe if you copy me."

As I slithered behind Kano toward the cave wall, two things were on my mind: I had to do what he said until I figured out how things worked in Aventurine, and learning to shape-shift without help was my first priority. The sooner I could change back into my normal self, the better.

5

Slither and Puff

Being a snake wasn't as icky as I first thought. Most of my overlapping yellow and green scales were dry and smooth. The rough scales on my underside gripped the rock ·floor, which helped me move and control my direction. My belly was also supersensitive to vibration. I could feel Kano moving ahead of me. Even better, I could tell if something snuck up behind me. At the moment, we were alone in the cave.

"Did you eat the cake so you could shift, too?" I asked.

Kano paused at the wall and raised his head to look back. "No, I jusssst like cake. I've alwayssss been able to shift."

"Issss that why Queen Patchouli picked you to guide me?" I asked.

"A shape-shifter wassss required," Kano said.

If Kano were a natural shape-shifter, I began to wonder if his real form was the hot guy or if that was simply another pattern he had mimicked. He'd given me such a hard time about commenting on his looks, I didn't want to ask point-blank. I tried to be sneaky.

"Why do we have human eyessss?" I asked.

"It'ssss the trademark of a shape-shifter. The one thing we can't change," Kano said. "No one knowssss why, but I'm glad that it'ssss sssso. Ssssometimessss it'ssss good to have a reminder of your true form."

That was a deeper response than I'd expected. It answered part of my real question at least, though: Kano's gorgeous eyes were definitely real.

I was quiet as I thought about what he'd said. Did shape-shifters ever forget that they were human? Is that what he meant about needing a reminder? When I was younger, I had dreamed of being able to change into any animal I wanted. What kid hadn't? I'd always wanted to be a bird. Flying would be amazing! It was too bad we were underground and I was stuck mimicking Kano. How cool would it be to shift into a bird, just like my childhood fantasy? I guess I might love it so much, I wouldn't want to change back. That must have been what Kano meant about remembering our true form. If so, this power was totally awesome and a little scary.

Kano's tongue flicked constantly as he moved. So did mine. The nonstop slurping in and out was irritating until I realized my tongue was also my nose! Teensy bits of everything in the air collected on my tongue. Receptors in my mouth analyzed the chemicals so I would know when food or enemies were nearby. I sensed traces of cake and icing along with dirt, microbes, seaweed spores, and Kano's soap.

I realized something else about snakes. They ate mice by swallowing them whole. I almost puked.

"I don't want to eat any little furry thingssss," I said.

"We're black rock ssssnakessss. In Aventurine, the only furry thingssss we eat are fungussss and mold." Kano stuck his head in a small hole in the wall for a few seconds. Then he continued around the base of the cave wall.

I froze, completely grossed out by a mental picture of fuzzy blue-green fungus on crackers.

"I can't eat mold, either," I said.

"I chosssse thissss form for a lot of reassssonssss," Kano said. "Black rock sssssnakessss don't have fangssss or venom, and they eat plantssss."

"Plantssss can't grow in cavessss," I said. "No ssssunlight."

Kano made a hiccupping hissing sound. He was laughing. "Anything can happen in Aventurine.

Thesssse cavessss are full of thorny toadsssstoolssss, lichen, and algae. Yum!"

"I'll sssstarve," I said.

"You won't be a sssssnake long enough to sssstarve." Kano turned to check out another hole.

Now that we were close to it, I could see that the cave wall was riddled with holes of different shapes and sizes. Most of them were too high to reach or too small for our foot-long snake bodies. The one Kano was investigating looked large enough, and it was only four inches up from the cave floor.

"I think I've found our way out," Kano said.

It suddenly occurred to me that Kano didn't really know where we were. "What if it issssn't?" I asked.

"Then we'll keep looking. Or we'll morph into rock wormssss and make our own tunnel. Their accccid eatssss through rock." Kano didn't wait for my response. He slithered into the hole.

When the tip of his tail disappeared, I rose up and peeked in. The round tunnel was barely wide enough to slide through. A few scattered crystals shed dim specks of light, but I could see Kano in the dark.

"You're lit up like an orange lightbulb!" I exclaimed. The effect was totally cool and reassuring. I wouldn't lose track of a guide who glowed in the dark.

"You have infrared vissssion," Kano explained.

"Your eyessss ssssee my body heat."

"I thought we were cold-blooded," I pointed out.

"Thissss issss Aventurine . . . !" Kano's voice trailed off as he sped away down the passage.

I slithered into the hole and hurried to catch up.

I'd never been claustrophobic, but the barely-big-enough tunnel put me on edge. I wished I knew where we were going and how long it would take to get there, but I didn't want to drive Kano crazy with too many questions. I just followed the orange glow and hoped we would arrive soon.

I spent the time thinking more about my new power. It still blew me away to think that when I learned to shape-shift on my own, I could be anything I wanted. The possibilities were endless—and not just for animal forms. I could see how I'd look with short hair—without having to cut a single strand! If I broke a nail, I could grow a new one. If the sensational shoes I just bought pinched, I could make my feet smaller. I could even age myself to see what I'll look like when I'm twenty-one.

Even better: What if I could morph myself wearing different clothes? Seeing how my designs looked on a real person would be priceless.

I mentally played with that idea until the narrow passage opened into a wider tunnel with more crystals and brighter light. Ahead of me, Kano continued moving forward without pause. My relief at leaving the tunnel didn't last long. The corridor smelled like something had died in it, and I could track the movements of strange creatures on the rock around me.

Glowing red rock worms wiggled in and out of small holes, eating light crystals and leaving acid grooves in the rock. I hoped Kano didn't really expect me to change into a worm if this path didn't take us out. White speckled round things covered with tentacles grew in clumps on the ceiling and walls. Slimy blue slugs with six feelers and twelve legs munched on the round things. Large, flat amoeba-like creatures clung to the rock like transparent splatters.

I watched in morbid fascination as one of the flat amoeba creatures suddenly engulfed a blue slug.

"I'm glad we're not thosssse thingssss," I said.

"Sssslickerssss are too sssslow," Kano explained, flicking his tail in dismissal at the amoeba creatures.

As we moved on, I wondered what my friends would say if they knew I was slithering through a cave in the body of a snake! Hisako and Eiko used to be part of my make-believe games when we were little. We had a lot of fun pretending to be ponies and other cute animals. Nobody ever pretended to be a snake.

I was jolted out of my daydreaming when the rock wall seemed to come alive. A lumpy head with snapping jaws popped out of the wall. It grabbed a slicker and sucked it down like a noodle. When I looked closer, I realized that dozens of holes in the wall had the creatures camouflaged inside.

"Watch out!" I called to Kano as he neared the large colony. Three heads emerged but quickly ducked back in as he passed by.

"Don't worry!" Kano called back. "Grabberssss won't bother ussss."

Although the rock creatures shrank back from me, I stayed alert. I didn't want to be surprised by something worse.

As we slid deeper and deeper into the rock, the grabbers and other life-forms began to thin out. Eventually, they were gone, and I noticed that the walls were damp and slick water covered the floor. The slippery surface made us move even faster.

At first, sliding through the tunnel was as much fun as the huge slides at a water park. The passage twisted and turned, and I sailed over bumps and down inclines. But when the tunnel leveled out, it began to fill with water.

"Turn back!" I shouted as I thrashed, trying to turn around. "We'll drown!"

"We won't drown!" Kano sounded exasperated.

"Black rock ssssnakessss can breathe underwat —
gurgle — blub!"

I struggled not to panic when the water covered my
head. Kano was my guide. He wouldn't deliberately
do anything to harm me, but he should have warned
me. Still, I was actually more annoyed at myself.

I'd always been a take-charge kind of girl. This
might not be my usual cup of tea, but I had to stop
acting like a helpless wimp. I waited until breathing
through my gills didn't feel strange. Then I whipped
in front of Kano and charged ahead.

"Let'ssss go, sssslowpoke!" I yelled. Now that we
were both submerged, we could talk again.

"Wait!" Kano shouted.

"No!" My underwater snake laugh sounded like
boiling water. "Catch me if you can!"

The speed was exhilarating. I was enjoying myself
so much, I didn't see the circle of gray light ahead
until it was too late to slow down or stop. I shot out of
the large tunnel into deep water.

And promptly began to sink.

In my mind, I paddled furiously to swim back up.
In reality, I didn't have arms or legs, and my wiggling
made me sink faster.

"Kano!" I tried to get a look at the bottom of the
water, but it was so deep, I couldn't spot it.

"Shout when you can ssssee me!" Kano called out.

I caught Kano's movement as he arrowed down through the gray water.

"I ssssee you!" I yelled.

Kano continued to plunge toward me. When our eyes locked, he suddenly transformed. One second he was a black rock snake. The next he was a round yellow puffer fish with spiky skin, a tiny puckered mouth, and green eyes.

"Fugu!" As I shouted the Japanese word, I began

to change. The process wasn't quite as clumsy as the first time, but it took me more than a few seconds. When I finished, I sank down below Kano again.

"Are you okay?" Kano yelled as he drifted down.

"No, I'm fugu!" I joked as I waved my tiny tail and fins and rose to meet him.

"What's a fugu?" Kano asked.

"A Japanese delicacy," I explained. "It takes a lot of training to make, and very few chefs get a license."

"What's a license?" Kano asked as we continued swimming upward, side by side.

It was cool being the one answering questions and not asking them. "It's a paper you get after you prove you can do something. Like drive a car or be a doctor. So other people don't get hurt," I added.

"Why do you need one to cook?" Kano asked.

"Because puffer fish are superpoisonous," I explained. "If fugu isn't prepared exactly right, it can kill you. People die every year."

Puffer fish only have one expression: a puckered mouth. I could only tell Kano was amazed by the sound of his voice.

"I don't understand why anyone would eat a fish that might kill them," he said.

"I don't, either." I would have grinned if I could. We agreed on something!

"Aventurine puffer fish aren't poisonous," Kano said.

"We aren't very good swimmers, either." I was moving my fins back and forth like crazy, but I just waddled through the water.

"I puffed up so you wouldn't sink so fast." Kano spat out a huge amount of water and instantly deflated.

I copied Kano, but being flatter didn't make much difference. Our spiky skin and tiny fins just weren't very efficient. That's why puffer fish blow up like balloons. They can't swim faster than a predator, but nothing wants to eat a poisonous ball of spines. Still, I wished Kano had picked a faster fish that wasn't so ugly.

We were getting along, and I didn't want to spoil it by questioning his judgment. I phrased my next question carefully. "Do you like being a puffer fish?"

"I'd rather be a silver sliver fish," Kano said, "but then we'd be stuck in this cave."

I was surprised to learn we were in another cave. I couldn't see the walls in the grayish water. Then I got nervous. "Why would we be stuck?"

"You'll see when we get to that ridge," Kano said.

The rock ahead was a blur that slowly came into focus as we approached. The cave wall wasn't solid. A three-foot-high opening broke the face of rock as far as I could see in both directions. Kano and I hovered just outside.

Crystals embedded in the ceiling lit up the interior of the huge horizontal crevice. A wavy blanket of purple, gold, green, red, and brown sea urchins covered the entire floor. Most of the urchins were smaller than an inflated puffer fish, and all of them were covered with spines. There were thousands, and the unbroken mass stretched into the distance.

"See that dark hole in the rock behind the urchins?" Kano asked. "That's the only way out."

I gasped. There wasn't enough clearance. A deflated puffer fish couldn't fit between the rock ceiling and the sea urchins.

"Do these things sting?" I asked.

"Yes, but they don't like puffer fish spines." Kano inhaled water until he was round again.

I hung back as Kano swam forward. As if by magic, the spiny round urchins rolled out of his way. I inflated and followed slowly, giving the little creatures time to clear a path. Halfway across, I saw a glint of light.

"What else lives in here?" I asked.

"Just the microbes and algae the urchins eat," Kano said.

"Do any of them light up?" I swiveled to scan the area. All I saw were sea urchins.

When the light flickered again, Kano yelled, "That's it!"

"What?" I asked. Then I realized what he meant. "Is it a mirror shard?"

"Nothing here shines like that," Kano said. "It must be a shard."

"Nice!" The light disappeared, but I focused on the spot and spoke the magic words: "Takara's truth!"

Nothing happened.

I'd expected the hand mirror to pop into view with a flash of golden light. Now I felt silly.

"What's wrong?" I sounded a little bit whiny, but I was too upset to care. "I said the words. Why didn't it work?"

Kano deflated slightly, as though he didn't have an answer, either. "Maybe you just have to be closer to the shard than you are now."

"Maybe." I exhaled with frustration. As soon as my body began to deflate, the sea urchins closed in. I quickly inhaled more water. "Or maybe it isn't a shard."

"You'll have to go look to be sure," Kano said. "The rest of your quest will be worthless if you leave the first shard behind."

He was right about that. I had to go.

I drew in more water to make sure I was as big and round as possible. The sea urchins wanted to avoid puffer fish as much as I wanted to avoid them, but there's a joker in every crowd. I didn't want to meet a sea urchin that thought it was tough or wanted a puffer for a big sister. As Okasan had told me over and over again, anything is possible in Aventurine.

As I inched my way toward the flicker of light, the creatures parted to let me pass. None of them wanted a fight, and I quickly came within a few inches of the glinting light.

I had found the first piece of the mirror!

The shard reflected my puffer face. The shard was triangular and wedged between three purple sea urchins with crisscrossing, interlocked spines. The sea urchins looked hopelessly tangled.

And they didn't budge when I got close enough to almost touch them.

For one brief, insane second, I thought about

trying to grow a pair of hands. Or claws! I even considered giving myself scales as protection against the sea urchins' spines. Then I imagined the mess I might become if I didn't do it right. My second transformation had gone smoother than the first, but Kano had given me a pattern to copy. If things went wrong, I could be paralyzed or stung to death before he reached me.

I was stuck being a puffer fish.

One of the dreaded enemies of sea urchins, I reminded myself. I gritted the little bit of teeth I had and stuck one of the purple pincushions with my spines.

The urchin couldn't get away fast enough! It pulled its spines free and rolled back. The threat of being touched pushed the other two clear, and the shard slowly fell into a bed of soft algae growing on the rock.

I hovered over the shard. It was mine!

"Takara's truth!" I shouted.

The hand mirror appeared in a brilliant burst of light and hung in the water before me. The shard shot off the rock and snapped into place in the frame. I stared, astonished, as the tarnish and grime vanished from the engraved brass around the restored glass. A long minute passed before I remembered that I had to send the mirror away again.

"Takara's truth." I puffed happily as the Yugen Lineage talisman disappeared. "Awesome," I whispered.

I swam back to Kano with renewed confidence.

"You did it!" Kano sounded as happy as I felt.

His happiness made me feel even better. I swished my fins and tail so fast that I swirled around in excitement. Then I realized he might not be happy *for* me. He might just be glad he was one shard closer to getting rid of me. I played it cool.

"It wasn't that hard." I didn't know why I had expected the task to be difficult. Everything from algebra to trimming bonsai came easily to me. "As soon as I can shape-shift into whatever I want whenever I want, this mission will be a snap."

"Don't be too sure," Kano said. "We just started."

"You worry too much." Taking the lead, I swam toward the exit of the cave. Behind me, I thought I heard Kano sigh.

6

A Tantalizing Trap

I liked the way the sea urchins parted before me as I swam toward the exit of the cave. They moved aside as if they were making way for a movie star. Funny how being a fat fish with a spiky skin condition could make me feel like a gorgeous celeb. I laughed.

Kano must have noticed the bubbles of laughter coming out of my mouth. "So you *are* enjoying yourself."

He sounded so smug, I bristled.

"No, I'm not! I can't wait to change out of this ugly form. I can't wait until I can change forms like I change clothes back home."

"Do you change clothes often?" Kano asked.

"Two or three times a day," I said.

"For survival," Kano stated matter-of-factly.

"For *style,*" I said. "No matter what I'm doing or where I'm going, I always dress with style."

Kano paused, puzzled. "What's style?"

"Style means . . ." I paused to think. Style wasn't easy to define. "It means doing something or creating something that stands out because it's unique or beautiful or the latest look."

"That doesn't sound very practical," Kano said.

It wasn't hard to figure out why Kano didn't understand. He changed into the best form for every situation, but he had no sense of artistry.

"Well, I don't completely ignore the weather. The seasons help determine the best styles, too. Like, I'll wear light sundresses in summer and knit sweaters in winter so I don't get too hot or too cold," I said. "I'll wear the latest fashions from Paris or New York or my own designs, but I always look great."

"Doesn't that depend on who's looking?" Kano asked.

"People always notice me," I said.

"It's not always good to be noticed," Kano said.

"It is if you want to be a fashion designer," I said as we reached the hole in the cave wall.

Kano hesitated before going in. The tunnel was only about twenty feet long. If we could swim faster, we'd reach the other end in a few seconds.

With the sea urchins behind us and a clear path ahead, there was no reason to delay. "Let's change into a faster fish now."

"Not yet," Kano said. "I don't know what's in the passage or what we'll find on the other side."

"You don't?" I was shocked. "Then how can you find Bristolmeir?"

"I drank a potion that acts like a compass. Queen Patchouli gave it to me," Kano explained. "I know what direction to take. I just don't know what we'll encounter along the way."

"You knew about the sea urchins," I said.

"Because Queen Patchouli told me," Kano said. "She knew we had to leave the first cave through a rock tunnel that would take us to the underwater cave. And she knew that sea urchins blocked the only exit."

"Then why didn't Queen Patchouli tell you what comes next?" I asked.

"She can't tell what she doesn't know," Kano said evenly. "Nothing is set from this point on. We might run into a surge current or a trench troll, or we might not. There's no way to know. We're going to have to be cautious and stick together."

"You're awfully calm about it." I was not calm. The idea of traveling through the weird underwater fairy world without any idea what to expect was not my idea of fun.

"I can transform to counter any danger in an instant," Kano said.

"But I can't." This time I was matter-of-fact. "My second shift was better than my first, but I was still too slow."

Kano waddle-swam in place without speaking. Suddenly his tiny fins became large fins.

My magically enhanced body grew bigger fins, too.

Next, Kano grew a long spine out of his forehead. The spine looked like what anglerfish use to lure smaller fish close enough to eat.

I automatically grew a long spine, and it happened a little faster. Kano was a good teacher. The best way to learn how to do something was to do it over and over again.

Then Kano added a luminescent yellow bulb on the end of the spine. "Make yours red," he said.

The bulb appeared without much difficulty, but I had to visualize red to change the color. It took me a few more seconds of heavy concentration.

"Is it red?" I asked.

"Yes," Kano said. "Now make it green."

For the next five minutes, Kano put me through my shape-shifter paces. We changed shapes, colors, and textures until I could copy Kano in an instant. However, Kano insisted that we should be puffer fish with angler lanterns while we traveled through the tunnel.

"You should follow me," Kano said as he slowly advanced. "In case I have to shift without warning."

I didn't argue.

The yellow bulbs dangling from our forehead spines cast a semicircle of light a foot or two ahead. I couldn't see the tunnel walls, but nothing moved in the water that filled the wide passageway. We reached the end without incident and swam out above another ledge.

Once again, Kano paused.

We were surrounded by a vast coral reef in hues ranging from pale yellow to bright orange and crimson red. I was happy to see that a puffer fish couldn't possibly fit through the narrow channels of the twisting labyrinth.

"It's so beautiful!" I exclaimed.

"It's dangerous." Kano spoke in a hushed voice, as though he didn't want anyone but me to hear.

Was he trying to scare me? Boys do that when they like a girl, but I didn't think that was Kano's reason. I was pretty sure he wanted to see what I would do. I tried not to freak out.

"In the waking world, some coral have stinging tentacles," I said. "Is that what you mean?"

Kano blinked with surprise. "Yes, except here the coral is also home to worms that bite."

It looked like the tunnel exit was deep within a

network of old coral, far from the vicious worms. Still, I wanted to be sure. "What do the worms look like?"

Kano instantly transformed into a creature that looked like a giant white maggot. His mouth had three sections. When the sections peeled back, a stalk with tiny snapping teeth popped out.

"No!" I squealed when I started to turn into the gross-looking worm.

Kano quickly turned into a small, slim blue fish with silvery striped scales and fins.

My body hesitated halfway through the worm transition and then copied the silvery blue fish.

"That's better!" I exclaimed. "This fish is very elegant, Kano. Thanks."

"I did not choose this form to please you, Sumi. The sliver fish is perfectly adapted to navigate through the coral."

"Then what are we waiting for?" Although my adventure had taken a turn for the better, I was still anxious to find the other shards so I could get back to my real life. "Let's go!"

"Wait!" Kano yelled. The warning held me back. "Coral has sharp edges. Even a sliver fish can get sliced open if it gets too close."

I waited.

Kano swayed in the water, looking to the right and left, up and down. I realized he was getting directions from the compass potion he had swallowed. Finally, he said, "We must go down to reach Bristolmeir."

That made sense. Queen Kumari had told me that Bristolmeir was at the bottom of the sea. I followed Kano into the coral maze, relieved to be moving forward again.

At first, I had to concentrate on steering through the lacy coral. But then I got used to my new speed and agility and started to take in the sights.

I was amazed at how much life thrived in the coral. Wispy blue grasses and green seaweeds with twining leaves swayed in the gentle currents. Pink and white urchins stuck to the coral like buttons, and schools of little red and yellow ribbonfish wove in and out of the columns. Sparkling sapphire and ruby-red starfish nestled in clumps of sea anemones, and translucent jellyfish clung to the underside of high coral arches. The jellyfishes' multicolored tentacles dangled like beaded curtains.

I began to imagine a whole line of clothes inspired by the life in the reef around me: the Sumi Hara Neptune Collection. When I first saw Queen Kumari, I had taken a mental picture of her silver gown. A shorter version with beaded detailing at the neck and long, wide-at-the-wrist sleeves would look fabulous with my long black hair. It was the first design I would try on when I perfected my shape-shifting ability.

"Watch out!" Kano shouted. "Those clams don't eat sliver fish, but if they catch a fin, it will hurt."

Off to the side, I saw dozens of blue clams. Their shells, which snapped open and closed to trap tiny green shrimp, sounded like music. To be safe, I tucked my fins in as we passed by.

As soon as we left the clams behind, Kano warned me of another hazard. "There's a colony of bell shells just ahead."

I heard a faint clinking sound, like water wind chimes. "Are they a problem?"

"They make the bell sound as they fall," Kano explained. "And they hit hard when they reach bottom."

"Where is the bottom?" I looked down. The mass of intertwining coral was just as thick underneath us as it was above.

"Bottom is anything that breaks the fall." Kano whipped his tail aside to avoid being struck. "You don't want that to be you."

A shell almost scraped my side as it dropped and shattered on the coral below. Another fell in front of me, then another off to the side.

My sliver fish instincts were sharper than my human ability to react. I ducked and darted through the rain of shells without being hit and somehow managed to avoid the knifelike edges of the coral, too.

The danger lasted only a minute, but it was a long, scary minute.

"I never want to do that again!" I exclaimed.

"Me neither!" Kano agreed. "If we run into another colony, let's try to swim around."

"Why didn't we swim around this one?" I asked.

"And miss all that excitement?" Kano teased.

"Yeah, excitement," I said sarcastically, and shot him a playful look to show I wasn't really mad.

Suddenly I wanted to take a detour. There was an irresistible smell that I just had to follow. I couldn't explain it, and I couldn't ignore it. I turned left into another channel. It was risky to go off alone, but my sliver fish instincts overrode everything else.

Golden eels with feathery blue tails swam leisurely in and out of stubby plants. They ignored me as I swam toward the source of the smell: a pile of eel eggs. I was starving! The feeling was so intense, I forgot to be cautious. When I darted into the secluded alcove to snatch the eggs, an eel turned on me with its razor-sharp teeth. I felt the teeth pierce my side, and in shock and pain, I struggled to get away from the eels and the sharp coral that seemed to be closing in around me.

"Sumi!" I heard Kano's voice in the distance. "Where are you?"

"Here . . . !" I cried out in a raspy whisper, my

voice fading along with my strength. I pushed myself to swim away from the eels' den, but then, too weak to swim any farther, I began to drift.

"Oh no!" Kano appeared next to me. I hadn't noticed him swim up. He gently nudged me away from the coral.

I expected him to yell, and I wouldn't have blamed him for being mad. Queen Patchouli had chosen him to guide and protect me. If I died in the reef, he'd be in trouble. But it would be my fault for leaving without telling him.

"An eel got me," I said. "I'm sorry I—"

"Don't talk," Kano said softly. "Save your strength." He formed a suction cup on his belly and anchored himself. Then he elongated his fins and held me while he examined the wound. I could feel my body try to shift to match his form, but it wasn't possible. I was in too much shock.

"It's bad, isn't it?" I asked.

"It's not good, but it could be a lot worse," Kano said. "You're tougher than some old eel, right?"

"Right," I said. Despite Kano's calm assurance, he sounded worried. *Because my safety is his responsibility,* I wondered, *or is he starting to like me?* Either way, I wanted to apologize for messing up. "I shouldn't have left—"

"So don't do it again," Kano said.

"But if I don't make it . . ." I gasped when a stinging pain shot through me.

"Don't talk like that. There's a cure," Kano said. "Mushwort grows all over the seas of Aventurine," he continued. "It heals gashes like this. We'll find some when we get out of the reef."

"I can't swim," I whispered.

"You don't have to. Just relax and enjoy the ride," Kano said in a forced light tone. He transformed his tail into a curved sled and then carefully scooped me onto it.

I dozed as Kano swam through the treacherous reef and woke when the clear water dimmed into a gloomy gray. The coral was newer, darker in color, and more densely packed. Here and there I saw the tip of a white worm emerge to snag pieces of seaweed or ocean bugs. I was too sick to be disgusted, but I tensed when Kano entered a narrow passageway. There were no outlets, and we barely fit, but he was prepared. He became thinner and wrapped his tail tighter around me until he swam clear.

"How long?" I asked as Kano's tail loosened.

"I smell mushwort not far ahead," Kano said, "but it might be difficult to reach."

"Why?" I asked.

"We're not alone," Kano said.

I peeked out and then immediately cringed back into the protective curl of Kano's tail.

A horrible creature stood between us and open water. With a bumpy sea horse head, spiraling horns, four snapping lobster claws, and a hooked scorpion tail, it looked like the *awabi* I had imagined when I was younger. My father, not being of the Yugen Lineage or knowing the legends of Aventurine, would sometimes tell me Japanese myths. The *awabi*, sea monsters that eat drowned fishermen and guard giant shells full of treasure, were one of his favorite characters.

"The *awabi* don't spend their profits, and they don't let anything go to waste," my father would say with an amused laugh. "The *awabi* understand good business."

This *awabi* didn't look like he cared at all about expense reports—he just wanted to kill us.

"What are we going to do?" I asked.

"I could change into a bottom crab," Kano said. "They have scissor claws that are very quick. I could fight the creature, but I don't think I'd be big enough to win."

"Then change into something faster," I suggested. "I don't have the energy to transform, but maybe you could lure the creature away."

"Perhaps I could, but you can't swim to safety," Kano said. "Something else might be out here waiting for a chance to attack. I won't leave you alone."

His human eyes met mine—they were filled with worry and determination. Before we entered the reef, I would have thought Kano's concern was just a matter of duty. Now his determination to stay and protect me seemed like something one friend would do for another. Either way, I wouldn't let him get hurt because I had done something stupid. There had to be another way out besides fighting or running.

The monster glared at us with glittering yellow eyes, waiting for us to make a move.

I always liked Okasan's tales better than my father's, but now I was glad I had listened to him, too. I didn't see any shells full of gold and jewels, but the creature had to be guarding the way forward for a reason.

"Ask what it . . ." I couldn't finish. Trying to speak sent another stabbing pain shooting through my side.

Kano understood. He faced the monster and asked, "Who are you?"

"I am Argo of the Not-Too-Deep," the creature bellowed.

Kano didn't show fear. "What do you want?"

"I want to eat you!" Argo's booming laugh sent ripples through the water. "I have not feasted on sliver fish in ages."

"And you will not eat sliver fish today!" Kano instantly transformed into a bloated fish with tough skin and warts.

"A toadfish!" Argo roared. "They taste terrible!"

Kano stopped his tail from shifting to match his new body, but not before Argo caught a glimpse of me.

"What are you?" Argo demanded. "And what's that in your tail?"

"I am a shape-shifter in the service of Queen Patchouli of the Willowood Fairies," Kano explained. "I have been charged with taking Sumi Hara to Bristolmeir."

Argo thrust his lumpy snout forward, tasting scent in the water. He relaxed his snapping claws and swished his tail uncertainly. "I know of this fairy queen. Is Sumi Hara a fairy-godmother-in-training?"

"She is," Kano said, "and she was wounded in the coral. If I don't get her to mushwort soon, she'll die."

"Queen Patchouli would be angry," Argo said.

"Yes," Kano agreed.

"That would not be good for me," Argo muttered. His body heaved in a resigned sigh. "All right. You may pass."

"Thank you," Kano said. "I will make sure Queen Patchouli knows of your kindness."

As a precaution, Kano didn't change his toadfish

form. He swam a slow but steady course toward the mushwort.

To take my mind off the pain, I closed my eyes and thought about my line of ocean clothes. There should be lace detailing on some pieces to match the coral.

The farther we got from Argo, the stronger the stench of onion breath and sour milk became. I didn't have the strength to complain and just focused on inventive uses for lace.

"We're here." Kano stopped and lowered his tail.

I gasped as he gently set me down by a pit of green oatmeal goo. Foul-smelling vapors rose off the bubbling surface, and nothing but slime weed grew nearby.

"Just get in," Kano said. "You'll start feeling better right away."

"I am *not* getting in that." I mustered the energy to sound as serious as I felt.

"You have to if you want to live." Kano wasn't joking.

"There's no other way?" I asked.

"None," Kano said. "Mushwort is the only cure."

I told myself it would be like taking a mud bath at an exclusive spa. Still, I whimpered with more than just pain as I slid off the slimy weeds into the green glop. I expected the ooze to be hot. It was cold, and just as Kano had said, the pain subsided when the chilly substance touched my injured side.

"It's working!" I shouted from the center of the pool.

"I know!" Kano called back.

I didn't care if he gloated a little. The pain eased as the gash began to close, and I sank into the mushwort with a sigh of relief. That was when I felt something hard bump up against me.

I wasn't alone.

7

Plant Tricks and Fish Treats

I thrashed in the mushwort to get away from whatever was lurking in the pit.

"What's wrong?" Ignoring the odor and fumes that kept other fish away, Kano swam toward me.

"Something else is in here!" I frantically looked around, expecting something to bite me or pull me under. I didn't see anything at first. Then something jagged and goo-covered bobbed to the top. It was hard to tell, but I thought it might have been shard number two.

"Takara's truth," I said.

The Yugen mirror appeared in a burst of dazzling light. As the shard shot out of the pit, the green goo peeled away. The shard snapped into place with a satisfying click.

"That's two!" I transformed one of my fins into a thumb and gave Kano a thumbs-up.

"Nice work!" Kano grinned.

The expression on his bumpy toadfish face was so comical, I laughed. My side didn't hurt at all.

I felt refreshed and energized when I swam out of the pit. My wound was completely healed. My side didn't even have a scar.

When I swam next to Kano in his toadfish form, my body immediately started to change. I fought the impulse to copy him. After being attacked and dunked in really gross, smelly stuff, I didn't want to be a plump fish with warts. I smoothed out the bumps and kept my slim sliver fish figure, but the struggle drained some of my recovered strength.

"Are you staying like that?" I asked Kano. "Toadfish aren't even a little bit cute."

"But they taste like mud and burn your mouth," Kano said. "That's why we're not digesting in Argo's stomach."

"Argo's gone now," I pointed out.

"Yes, but it takes too much energy to shift for no reason," Kano said.

I opened my mouth to argue, but it was true, and I didn't want to admit I was using my reserves to be a pretty fish. Kano was such a boy. He'd never understand that girls need to do a lot of unreasonable things to look nice. He'd probably tell me I was foolish and vain. That wouldn't be new. I've been called vain before, but it never bothered me. Jealous people are quick to call names.

Kano was different. He clearly didn't envy me or anyone else. He didn't need to. Kano could choose his appearance down to the finest detail. If he wanted, he could be a tall, dark, handsome human with silky hair, flawless skin, and perfect white teeth. He just didn't care how he or anyone else looked. He valued form and function. I'd never met anyone like him— except maybe Okasan, I realized.

A wart popped up on my snout. I tried to ignore it, and I might have been able to if the blemish had been on my back. But it wasn't. It was right on the tip of my nose, like a horrible pimple I couldn't stop watching. I pushed it back down and swam without looking at Kano, which helped me control the impulse to change. I was still a sliver fish when we swam over a ridge into a field of green seaweed.

The plants grew on a slope that gradually descended deeper into the sea. Kano changed into a green fish that was wider top to bottom than a sliver fish but just as thin, with a longer tail and fins. He blended into the seaweed so perfectly, I couldn't see him for a moment. Without being able to see him, my body couldn't automatically copy the new shape, but the delay was an advantage. It gave me time to add a few Sumi Hara touches to Kano's basic design: Instead of pea-soup green, I picked an iridescent green with hints of blue, pink, and gold. I emphasized the rainbow effect in my longer fins and tail, adding diffuse pink and blue stripes flecked with gold.

"What is this?" Kano asked when I finished.

"This is style!" I swam in a tight circle, modeling my flashy fish fashion.

"Change color," Kano said. It sounded like a command.

I automatically resisted. "No."

"You're too visible in the seaweed," Kano explained with a hint of worry.

"That's the point!" I met his gaze and stood my ground. "I like to stand out."

"But you might attract something dangerous," Kano argued.

"If that happens, I'll change." My alterations to Kano's basic form had been easy enough. I could shift into dull green if I were threatened.

"If there's no warning—"

"I'll be fine!" I cut him off with a sharper snap than I intended and softened my explanation. "I can't wear the beautiful outfit Queen Kumari let me pick out because I have to be a fish. So I'm going to be a beautiful fish."

Kano snorted bubbles. He was annoyed.

I didn't want anything to ruin the little bit of joy I had found in Aventurine. I headed down the slope, leaving him behind to pout.

The motion of my flowing fins through the water felt wonderful, like the swish of the dress I wore to my first school dance. The dress was royal blue with sparkly sequins, and I'd stood out in a crowd of white and pastel pink. Everyone had told me that I looked gorgeous.

None of the ocean creatures I passed seemed dangerous at all.

Kano was worried for nothing, I thought smugly.

Although we were swimming deeper, the water stayed warm and teemed with interesting life. Long grassy seaweed dominated the scenery, but dozens of other plants grew on the ground around the slender stalks. Brown, green, and gray fish of various shapes and sizes swam through stands of matching foliage. A turtle with two heads, six legs, and a pointed shell wandered through clumps of small cabbage plants. It stopped when its heads wanted to go in opposite directions. After a brief struggle, the left head won, and I giggled as the turtle turned left and swam away. When I swam over a pile of flat black rocks, they turned into rays with wide, rippling wings and took off!

It dawned on me that unlike the creatures living in the coral reef, everything in the seaweed field was camouflaged to blend in.

Everything.

Maybe Kano was right to be worried about my color scheme? I took another look around.

Giant clams with jagged-edged shells were buried in the sand, waiting for anything to swim too close. The fuzzy green disks opened into huge mouths that sucked in small fish, shrimp, and jelly globes. What if something bigger and more ominous were hiding, waiting to strike?

I was too embarrassed to admit my mistake, but I wasn't foolish enough not to change. As I started to shift to the safety of boring old green, I was distracted by a glimmer of light. Was it the third shard? I couldn't be sure. The water wasn't as clear as it was in the sea urchin chamber or the coral reef. I swam toward the glint for a closer look.

"Where are you going?" Kano asked.

"I think I saw a shard!" I shouted, bursting with excitement. When shard number three was back in the mirror, I'd be more than halfway toward my goal.

"Where?" Kano asked as he swam after me.

"It's in that mass of seaweed." I pointed with a fin.

There was no doubt. The missing piece of mirror was in the leaves. I didn't have to navigate through stinging urchins or take a dip in foul glop to get it. The shard was just sitting there, waiting for me to summon Takara.

"Stop!" Kano called out as I sped toward the shard. He sounded panicked.

I was swimming too fast to stop suddenly, so two inches from the shard, I whipped into a turn and circled back toward Kano. I didn't see a threat and nothing seemed to be chasing me, but I didn't want to risk it when he sounded this concerned.

"What?" I gave a bewildered shrug with my fins.

Kano wasn't amused. "Maybe I *should* have let you swim into that carnivorous sea sponge. It might finally teach you a lesson."

"What carnivorous sea sponge?" I didn't see anything big enough to eat me.

"The one holding the mirror shard," Kano said. "It blends into the seaweed around it. That's how it tricks unwary prey."

Like me, I thought.

When I looked at the green mass now, I could see things I hadn't noticed at first glance. The giant sponge stood in a thick patch of seaweed, where its lacy flaps blended into the leaves. As I watched, a brown fish swam too close. Long spongy lip flaps shot out and snapped it up. The fish was gone in less than a second.

If not for Kano's warning, I would have been devoured. That possibility was a hundred times more frightening than being attacked by an eel. The eel had just been trying to protect her eggs, not actually eat me. The feeling of cold terror severed the last threads of my denial. Despite all the evidence, I had been dealing with my mission as if it were just a vivid dream. As if nothing could really hurt me. But I wasn't dreaming.

Aventurine was real. And so was the scary sea sponge that had my shard.

A mere two inches had saved me from being eaten like the unfortunate brown fish. I didn't want to go on.

But if I didn't finish my mission, I would dishonor my mother and the Yugen Lineage, and I'd be banished from the fairy world.

In the tradition of all Japanese heroes, death was better than dishonor.

"Thank you, Kano." I paused to hush the tremor in my voice. "I can't think of anything worse than being eaten."

"It's probably not fun," Kano joked, trying to calm me.

"Definitely not on my top-ten list of things to try,"

I added. I didn't want him to know I was afraid. "But I still have to get the shard."

Kano bobbed in the water, nodding. "You'll find a way."

I had to, or die trying.

I swam in a wide arc with a wary eye on the sponge's brown rolled-up lip flaps. After cautiously circling the camouflaged creature twice, I was certain it only had one mouth. There was less chance of being snagged if I approached the shard from the rear.

I didn't charge right in. I studied the lacy flaps that covered the sponge from a safe distance. Several fish swam by without being attacked. Putting off the task was pointless. I had to go for the shard quickly, before I lost my nerve.

With all my senses on high alert, I swam at the sponge from behind. When I came within a fish's length, I said the magic words. "Takara's truth!"

The brass hand mirror didn't appear.

I inched closer to the sponge and tried again, with no luck. I swam back to the front and realized that the shard was tangled in seaweed. I had to free it before the mirror could appear.

I backed up to ponder the problem.

I could grow teeth and eat the seaweed, but that would put me dangerously close to the sponge's mouth. What wouldn't a sponge be able to eat? I ran through all the different sea creatures I could imagine, when I finally struck on an idea.

I changed one of my fins into a very long crab leg and claw. With my new, indigestible tool, it took no time at all to pull the seaweed away from the shard. I called for the hand mirror, and it appeared in a flash of light. The third piece of glass quickly snapped into the frame.

"Takara's truth!" I sent the mirror away and changed my crab leg back into a fish fin. Then I turned my fish mouth into a goofy grin at Kano, who'd been circling anxiously behind me. "Three down, and two to go."

"If you live that long," Kano said.

He had a point. I wouldn't survive if I didn't start using common sense. I had been so intent on getting the shard, I had forgotten to fully change from my brilliant colors to plain green.

"Point taken," I said. I couldn't tell him that I had meant to change right before I noticed the shard. It sounded like a lame excuse, even to me. I quickly finished changing color.

I looked to Kano for his approval. But he wasn't

looking at me. He had a frozen, horrified expression.

"Kano?"

This seemed to shake him out of it. He screamed, "Big fish!"

The warning came too late. I turned and found myself staring down the gullet of a gigantic fish. It clamped its mouth closed around me.

Several thoughts raced through my mind. Each worse than the last. *I'm stuck in a disgusting fish mouth! I'm eaten! I'm dead!*

The fish's mouth heaved as it prepared to swallow. I knew if I went down its throat, I'd be a goner.

I desperately shifted into the first thing I could think of that would keep me from being swallowed: an octopus. It's another Japanese delicacy, like fugu, that is dangerous. Some people eat live octopus, but they have to do it just right, because if the octopuses use their suckers while you swallow, they'll choke you to death!

I quickly finished my transition into an octopus with sucker-covered tentacles and spread my many new legs around the inside of the fish's mouth. When its muscles contracted to swallow, I gripped hard and held on.

The fish tried several times to dislodge me. I

97

was stuck fast, but unlike the culinary daredevils who die eating live octopus, the fish didn't choke. It just kept trying to swallow me over and over again.

I waited for the fish to open its mouth, thinking I could make a break for it and swim clear. I was wrong. The instant the fish's mouth opened, I loosened my tentacles, and the fish shut its mouth and tried to swallow me again.

Staying braced in the beast's mouth was tiring. I knew I couldn't do it for long. I had to escape soon or I'd end up as lunch.

Growing too big to fit in the fish's mouth might work, except the fish would probably explode. Being covered in blown-up fish innards was grosser than soaking in mushwort but better than death. I filed the idea away as an option of last resort.

I considered turning my tentacle suckers into spines. If I jabbed the fish, it might want to get rid of me. To save energy, I tried one spine to test my theory. The inside of the fish's mouth was so hard, the spine broke off.

I had the awful feeling that I had just broken a nail. I'd find out when I turned back into a girl, if I ever did.

A horrific image of bubbling bile flashed before me. The thought of being slowly digested was so awful, I shuddered. The spasm caused me to squirt out a puff of black mist.

Of course!

I remembered reading that octopuses shoot out an inky black cloud to distract predators so they can flee. I just hoped the stuff tasted bad.

I thought about being digested again. My fear was so strong, I spewed enough inky black liquid to completely fill the fish's mouth.

It spat me out!

I quickly kicked my eight legs and swam away from my captor. When I was safely behind a pile of rocks, I changed into a dull green fish. I probably didn't look exactly like Kano, but my new form was close.

There were just two huge problems, I realized as the cloud of ink trailing behind me dissipated: I didn't see Kano, and I was no longer in the expansive field of green seaweed. I was in a deep underwater canyon.

Sheer cliffs towered above me, and there were rocks and boulders everywhere. The water was dark and much colder, and I saw no signs of life. While I had struggled inside it, the big fish had carried me really far off course.

"Kano," I whispered into the deep. I was still too terrified to bring attention to myself. After a few minutes of whispering Kano's name, I finally got up the courage to shout, "Kano! Where are you?"

"Coming!"

My tiny fish heart fluttered at the sound of Kano's voice. I peered through the gray water, expecting to see a green fish. Instead, I saw an even larger fish than the one I had just escaped. And it was swimming right for me.

8

Rocky Road and House Hunters

I was tired after the battle with the other big fish, but I had come too far to give up without a fight. The only reasonable course of action was to become something the fish couldn't eat.

I turned into a clam with a superhard shell.

"Wow!" the fish exclaimed. "That was a fantastic shift, Sumi."

Kano?

"You can change back into a fish now," Kano said. "The coast is clear."

When I transformed, the huge fish was hovering before me. I finally noticed Kano's liquid green eyes staring out at me. "Kano?"

"It's me!" Kano laughed.

Furious, I whipped my little green fish tail back and forth. "You scared me to death!"

"Sorry," Kano said as he changed back into his smaller fish form. "I had to transform into something big to keep up with the fish that caught you. He was really moving."

"I'm glad it's you," I said. "I've been almost eaten enough for one day."

"I'm glad you're okay." Kano sounded sincere. "I was worried. If I had lost you . . ." His voice trailed off, and I hurried to smooth over the awkward moment.

"It'll take more than a big fish for you to get rid of me," I said with a laugh. Despite the fact that we didn't see eye to eye on most things, I was starting to like the shape-shifter. I couldn't be sure if he felt the same about me, but I hoped so.

"Apparently," Kano said.

"So, on to the next shard. Which way to Bristolmeir?" I asked.

Kano turned in a slow circle, then paused. "I don't know."

"We're lost?" I was aghast. "What happened to your compass?"

"It's not working," Kano said.

I almost asked why not, but Kano probably didn't know, and getting mad wouldn't help. It wasn't his fault something had gone wrong with the potion.

"Maybe these cliffs are blocking the essence of Bristolmeir," Kano said.

"Should we go back?" I asked.

"No," Kano said. "We should follow the canyon floor."

"What if the canyon is just a dead-end trench?" I asked. The rocky ground sloped downward as far as I could see.

"Then we'll know that it wasn't the right way to go, which will help us find the actual right way," Kano explained. "Besides, there aren't any dead ends—we're shape-shifters. We can always turn into something that's equipped to keep going."

"Good point. Lead the way." As I spoke, I heard a rumbling that sounded like a distant freight train. "What's that noise?"

"Change now!" Kano transformed into what looked like a barracuda and sped off.

I copied Kano without a second thought. Rocks began to fall as I dashed after him.

Boulders crashed against the canyon walls, slammed into each other, and smashed on the ground. Pebbles and dirt exploded into the water. I swam with a terrified speed. A large stone nicked my tail as I followed Kano's zigzagging course through a maze of boulders, stone arches, and rock piles.

Schools of fish and other creatures I hadn't noticed before fled the rock slide with us. Reddish-brown eels, sea snakes, and small sharks swam together. For the moment, the only enemy was the falling rock.

"Over here!" Kano called out as he ducked into a crevice in the cliff. I followed him into the crack.

It rained rocks for several minutes, and every time the cliff shuddered I was sure we'd be buried alive. I was consoled knowing that Kano and I could change into any shape necessary to save ourselves, but I felt sorry for the canyon creatures that couldn't.

When the thunderous sound of the rock slide stopped, Kano motioned that we should wait. For another long minute, we listened to isolated impacts as straggling boulders hit the ground. Then he waited another minute to make certain it was safe.

The canyon looked very different when we emerged. It was wider, and the ground behind and ahead of us was covered with boulders and rock piles.

"Are we barracuda?" I asked.

"Close. We're spiny darts. We look a lot like barracuda, but we have patches of barbed bristles. Your spines will eject if you're attacked," Kano said.

"Like a porcupine!" I thought Kano had made a wise choice, and I relaxed as we swam away from the falling-rock zone. I assumed we were safe now. But as we traveled deeper, something else became obvious.

We were puny compared to the creatures that inhabited the depths of the dark canyon. Everything else was supersized.

Clams were as big as houses. The smallest fish could swallow a car, and the seaweed looked like giant trees.

"How soon before we get out of here?" I whispered, hoping nothing could hear me.

"Scared?" Kano teased.

"Yes!" I hissed.

"Good. Me too," Kano whispered back. "Maybe you'll be more careful. I'm getting used to having you around."

I was so surprised, I couldn't think of anything to say. It sounded like Kano was starting to like me back! I smiled and swam a bit closer to him. It was nice to know that he was nervous, too. The threat of being eaten was like a common bond that drew us closer together and made our differences less important. The rest of the mission might be more fun because of it.

If we get out of this canyon, I thought.

A crunching noise made me turn to scan the water behind us. At first, I didn't see anything moving through the forest of brown sea ferns and dead tree trunks that had collected on the canyon floor over time. Then an army of silvery black lobsters with three claws stampeded by.

"What are they doing?" I asked Kano.

"Running!" Kano exclaimed with a burst of speed.

I ventured another glance back as we passed the lobsters.

A monstrous bulldozer of a fish charged toward us, scooping up everything edible in its path. With long, wiggling whiskers; black and green mottled skin; and a wide mouth with several rows of teeth, it was the ugliest and most terrifying creature I had seen so far, including Argo and the fish that had tried to eat me! The bulldozer fish wouldn't try to swallow me whole. It would pulverize me first. The fish was so much bigger and faster than a spiny dart—we couldn't outrun it.

"Go up!" Kano swam upward as fast as he could.

I followed, but I hadn't saved enough energy. I'd shifted too many times.

I used up my reserve just as the massive bottom-feeder caught up to us. It was useless. I gave one last surge of energy—completely desperate now—and screamed as I felt something brush against my belly.

It was the bulldozer fish's dorsal fin. I had made it far enough up for the fish to pass beneath me. It didn't stop—I was way too small to distract it from the smorgasbord of goodies on the canyon floor.

Kano slowly descended. "What happened?"

"I ran out of gas," I said. "We haven't stopped

moving since we left the first cave. I need to rest."

"We should eat, too," Kano said, "but not here. Can you keep going for a while longer?"

"Yes." I was exhausted and scared, but Sumi Hara doesn't give up. I would do whatever was necessary to survive.

We swam on for a long time. I kept expecting Kano to spot a cave and tell me to duck inside. In the meantime, I scanned the area for more big fish. The next problem, however, didn't sneak up on us. A mass of giant blue, white, and green jellyfish clogged the canyon ahead. I couldn't see the tops of the huge balloon-like creatures, and their paralyzing tentacles hung down to the canyon floor.

"Can we swim over them?" I asked Kano.

"We could, but we don't have to. Just follow me and fire at will."

Baffled, but trusting Kano's judgment, I swam behind him toward the menacing mass of jellyfish. When he reached them, he released a spray of bristles. The tentacles drew up, and Kano swam under them. I did the same, and my own bristles kept the tentacles at bay until I was safely through. Still, I felt bad about hurting something just to save time.

Kano saw my concerned look.

"The jellyfish will be fine," he said. "Dart bristles sting, but they dissolve quickly."

The animals on the far side of the clog of jellyfish were less frenzied, as though they knew the supergiants couldn't pass the barrier. Everything was still big, but not as dreadful or threatening. Orange and green fish swam in leisurely schools.

Kano didn't change out of his spiny dart suit. He slowed the pace and spoke. "I thought that first big fish had eaten you for sure. How did you get away?"

"I thought I was eaten, too," I said. "I was terrified, but then I thought about fugu."

"Oh!" Kano exclaimed. "You turned into a puffer fish."

"No, I turned into an octopus," I said. "The same people who think it's cool to eat poisonous fugu will eat live octopuses whole."

"Do they die doing that?" Kano asked.

"All the time," I said. "The tentacles get stuck in their throat and they choke."

Kano snorted his displeasure. "So you choked the fish?"

"Sort of," I said. "I used my tentacles to stick to the inside of its mouth so it couldn't swallow me. Then I sprayed ink."

"You did *what*?" Kano asked.

I giggled. "Well, it got the fish to spit me out."

Kano laughed. "You're a very clever and brave girl, Sumi Hara."

"Who's really sick of being a fish," I admitted. "I would love to be my real self again, even for just a few minutes."

I expected Kano to object, but he surprised me.

"Your wish is my command," he said.

He wasn't making fun of me. He gestured to something up ahead. There was a gigantic tapered shell by the cliff. Although it was as big as my Manhattan apartment building, I hadn't noticed it until he pointed it out. The spiraling shell was almost completely hidden under a mass of plants and rocks.

"It's huge!" I exclaimed as my gaze traveled upward. "I can't see the top."

"If the top breaks the surface of the water, there might be air pockets," Kano said as he swam inside. "If there are, you can be a girl until it's time to move on."

I didn't dare hope as I followed him into the shell.

So many things had taken up residence, I realized the original inhabitant had vacated the shell a very long time ago. Colorful algae, anemones, and seaweed were anchored to the floor, ceiling, and walls of the large lower chamber. Iridescent slugs cast a glow, making it easy for us to avoid fat sea worms.

On the far side of the chamber, we entered a

narrow, twisting passage that led to the next level. There were fewer light slugs in the curved corridor, and I tried not to think about the creepy things lurking in the dark. I tensed when Kano paused, but we weren't in danger. We had reached the threshold of an air chamber.

"The water level ends here," Kano said. "We have to leap out of the water onto the ledge, so be ready to change."

"I'm ready." I created a picture of myself in my mind. I had only worn the beautiful fairy clothes for a few minutes, but I knew exactly what they looked like.

Kano backed up, rushed forward, snapped his tail, and jumped. His slim fish body burst through the surface and vanished.

I was so anxious to transform, I threw myself out of the water and plopped on the shell floor. I landed so hard, I was dazed and disoriented. I caught sight of Kano. He had turned into a seal with sleek fur, whiskers, and flippers. The automatic copying process immediately changed me into a matching seal with lungs and a nose. But the instant I could breathe out of the water, I took control and continued shifting. In a single fluid transformation, I changed from fish to seal to girl.

After taking a few deep breaths, I laughed, spread

my human arms, and twirled. My long hair whipped around, and the silky fabric of my gray-blue dress swished against my legs. I wiggled my toes and stared, as though bare feet laced into leather sandals were an amazing sight. After the last few hours, they were.

Although I had adapted the instincts of the snake and the fish, being a girl was the only form that felt right.

"You've become an excellent shape-shifter," Kano said as he pulled himself across the hard floor on seal flippers.

"And you're adorable," I teased.

I tried to hide my disappointment that he hadn't shifted back to the gorgeous boy I had first met. I was a little surprised by how strongly I wanted to see the human Kano again. Dozens of boys had liked me, but I'd never been interested in a particular guy before. Kano was funny and caring and courageous—not in a macho, big-shot way, but for real.

"Do you like being a seal?" I asked.

"Who doesn't like warm, fuzzy things?" Kano said.

I almost said I wanted to snuggle with him, but that would have been too bold, even for me.

The air chamber was dimly lit by phosphorescent algae growing on the damp walls, and my human eyes quickly adapted to the low light.

"Why doesn't anything live here?" I asked.

"Because there's seawater below and freshwater rain pools in the chambers above," Kano explained. "A few life-forms can survive in both, but most can't."

I was so glad to be me again, a minute passed before I noticed water dripping off the ceiling. It wasn't just a few drops here and there. It was a steady drizzle.

"I'm ready to move on," I said. "My hair and clothes are getting wet."

"Wait here." Kano waddled to the spot where the spiral passage continued upward. After a quick glance into the opening, he said, "You're too big to fit through. If you want to go up, you have to change into something smaller."

"But I just became a girl again," I complained. "I don't want to be anything else so soon." The chamber was barren except for small pools of water, piles of brown seaweed, and the glowing algae. It wasn't comfortable, but it was safe. "Let's just stay here."

"That's okay with me," Kano said. "Seals love being wet!"

"I don't," I mumbled. Water was dripping off my hair and running down my cheeks. Within the next few minutes, my beautiful clothes would be soaked. "There must be a dry spot in here somewhere."

"Sorry. There isn't," Kano said. "I have an idea, but you probably won't like it."

"Will it keep me dry?" I asked.

"It will keep you from getting wetter," Kano said. "Change your hair into a big toadstool cap."

I grimaced at the thought.

"It will work," Kano said.

I imagined my gorgeous hair turning into a black toadstool. The thought of being a fungus grossed me out, but Kano's idea worked as promised. Now the water dripped off the edges of my toadstool umbrella.

"I like it," Kano said.

I wasn't surprised. Kano liked anything that served a useful purpose.

However, my sense of accomplishment didn't last long. The cool air felt colder against my damp skin, and the chill went through my lightweight clothes. I took the silver scarf from around my neck and draped it over my shoulders like a shawl, but I couldn't stop shivering. The scarf was too flimsy to keep me warm.

"Are you cold?" Kano asked.

"A little," I said through chattering teeth. "Aren't you?"

Kano shook his head. "I have a fur coat that's designed to keep me warm in cold water."

"A fur coat would be nice," I said.

"Just grow fur where you need it," Kano said. "White winter bears have thick coats."

Adding patches of white fur to my body was a bigger challenge than changing the shape and texture of my hair. I concentrated on my arms, starting at the wrists. Once the thick fur began to appear, it was easier to grow, and I didn't stop at my bare arms and legs. I grew a short coat under my clothes. The warming effect was instant.

"That's better!" I took a deep breath and exhaled with satisfaction. After all my underwater ordeals, being warm, dry, and human was a big relief. That didn't last long, either.

I grimaced again.

"Now what?" Kano sounded puzzled, not impatient or irritated.

"What's that smell?" I gagged. I was a girl.

Kano lifted his black seal nose and sniffed. "Rotting seaweed and decomposing dead things."

Piles of ocean debris were scattered throughout the chamber. I was getting more tired with every new alteration to the basic Sumi Hara design, but I wouldn't rest with the stench of compost in my nose.

This time, I didn't ask for Kano's advice. I flattened my nose, made my nostrils smaller, and added hairs to filter out the offensive particles. When I drew a breath, the odor was tolerable.

"I'm done!" I grinned, pleased with my progress as a shape-shifter. "Is the freshwater okay to drink?"

"It should be." Kano scooted over to a pool near the shell wall. He sniffed, then sampled the water. "It's good."

When I leaned over to get a drink, I caught a glimpse of myself before the water rippled and the image was gone. I looked ridiculous, and I burst out laughing.

"What's funny?" Kano asked.

"I look like a furry mushroom with a squashed cartoon face!" I doubled over in a fit of giggles.

"At least you're warm and dry and you can't smell anything," Kano said.

"You're all those things, too," I pointed out, "but you're a lot cuter."

It was true. A seal really was the perfect form to take while resting in the chamber. I had just wanted to hold on to Sumi the girl for a little while longer.

"Cute doesn't matter. It's all about comfort," Kano said.

"I know, but I think I'll give up my Frankenstein look and just be a seal." I struggled to keep down the giggles and lost.

Kano blinked his green eyes, twitched his whiskers, and made a throaty barking sound. I was pretty sure he was grinning.

"Great, but be a smaller one." As Kano spoke, he

reduced his size by half. "Then we can check out the upper chambers. They might be more comfortable."

"Is there any chance we'll find the fourth shard in here?" I asked as I transformed into a darling miniseal. I was instantly aware that the awful smell didn't smell awful. I wasn't cold, and I didn't mind being dripped on.

"This is Aventurine . . . ," Kano said.

"Everything is possible," I finished with him. We both laughed.

The next chamber was slightly smaller, with a large depression that covered almost the entire floor. Freshwater had collected in the bowl.

"We should swim across," I suggested. "It would be easier than walking around."

"That's a good idea," Kano said, "as long as you don't mind swimming with some big puddle beasties."

I took a closer look. The pool was swarming with creatures that looked like gigantic bacteria.

"I'll walk." I led the way around the pool, staying as close to the outer wall as possible in case any of the beasties were jumpers.

As we traveled upward, the chamber gradually became less stark and more welcoming. Smaller water pools were inhabited by tiny see-through crystal fish, blue frogs with bulging yellow eyes, and a variety of water bugs and plants. Cushy moss and lichen covered the mounds and ledges that time and water had carved into the shell walls.

Our exploration was stopped at the exit from the seventh chamber. The interior of the passage through the tapered shell tower had eroded into an impassable honeycomb.

"But what if the fourth shard is up there?" I had looked for the telltale glint in every chamber we had passed through. I was positive we hadn't missed it.

"It's not," Kano said with conviction. "The shards might be difficult to reach when you find them, but they won't be impossible to obtain. The fourth shard must not be here."

Kano's certainty helped but didn't entirely ease my nerves. It seemed like forever since I had found the third shard in the sponge. I had been through so much since eating the fairy cake—failing to completely assemble the Yugen Lineage mirror was too depressing to think about.

"Are you hungry?" Kano asked.

The question took my mind off the mission. "Starved, but after being a fish, I can't eat one."

"I found something better." Kano slid over to a ledge of layered rocks and smacked something with his flipper.

The enticing aroma of warm bread and butter filled my nostrils and made my mouth water. I ate the spongy stuff that grew on the ledge. I decided not to ask what it was. Better just to enjoy the meal.

Warm and dry with full stomachs, we curled up in a moss-covered corner and slept.

I awoke with a start, thinking I was home in my own bed. I only had to blink once to orient myself to the fantastic fact that I was a fairy-godmother-in-training in seal form in a monster shell in the Aventurine Sea.

The next blink alerted me to the strange sound that had disturbed my rest. I had heard something like it before, when Okasan had taken me to Central Park a few days after we arrived in New York. The chittering noise outside the alcove sounded exactly like a bunch of squabbling squirrels.

Kano opened his eyes and yawned as I peeked out of our corner. "What's going on?" he asked.

The feet and claws of a hundred small hermit crabs were clickety-clacking on the hard floor as they scurried around a heap of shells. I watched, fascinated, as a crab crawled out of one shell and into another. After a moment, he traded the second shell for a third shell that was slightly larger. Most of the other crabs were also trying on new shells for size and comfort.

"A bunch of hermit crabs are house hunting," I said.

It had never occurred to me that animals could

be just as particular about their shells and nests as I was about my clothes. It made me smile to think that shopping was a basic instinct in all of us. And it made me feel less alone.

The thought jolted me.

Was I lonely?

It was really hard to admit, but maybe I was. And not just because I was separated from my friends in Japan or because my parents both had busy careers or because I didn't know anyone in New York yet. This was bigger than that somehow. Maybe by always looking for attention and putting my life first, I had sort of cut myself off from people.

I shouldn't have blown off Hisako. She'd just wanted to talk about her new crush. I felt terrible. Then I remembered that Queen Kumari had said I'd return home the morning after the night I left. I'd be a little late getting in touch with Hisako, but not too late to ask about Akiyo.

A gravelly noise in Kano's throat distracted me.

"Are you growling or laughing?" I asked.

"Growling," Kano said. "I don't like what those big crabs are doing to that little crab."

I quickly picked out the small crab Kano was watching. Every time it found a shell it liked, a bigger crab came along and took the shell away.

119

"We have to do something!"

Kano nodded in agreement, but added, "You can't stop the big crabs from stealing the little crab's shells after we're gone."

"I think I can." I gave him a mischievous seal smile.

"Can't wait to see." Kano kept close behind me as I crept out of the niche.

The hermit crabs were too intent on bickering over shells to pay us much attention. As I started to look through a pile of seaweed for a suitable shell, one fell out of a hole in the wall and rolled up to my flippers.

"That's how all this small stuff gets down here," Kano explained. "It washes through the holes until it lands and stops."

"I guess that's why there's less stuff in the lower chambers." I picked up the shell. "Can I talk to hermit crabs?"

"If they want to talk to you," Kano said.

The small crab was huddled under a broad seaweed leaf, and I motioned for him to come over.

"No." The crab hissed. "I'm naked."

"I have a new shell for you that no one else will want," I said.

"If no one else wants it, why would I?" the crab asked, but he held on to the seaweed for cover and scooted closer. He looked at my shell and hissed again. "That's the worst shell I've ever seen!"

"He's right, you know," Kano whispered.

I smiled. Taking a hint from Okasan, I had chosen a shell that was chipped, stained with tar, and marred by barnacles.

"Just try it," I told the crab. "Walk around. See how it feels. If you don't like it, you don't have to keep it."

The crab hesitated, then let go of the leaf and slipped into the ugly shell. When it was adjusted to his liking, the crab walked around. "It's a good fit," he conceded.

"It's a lot better than that," I pointed out. "You've been wearing that shell for a whole minute, and no one has tried to take it away."

The little crab stiffened. "You're right!"

"Where I come from, the chip and the barnacles and the tar make that shell unique. That's why it's beautiful and very, very valuable."

My whiskers twitched with delight at how happy the crab was as he paraded around in his new shell. I turned to give Kano a smiling look, but he seemed disturbed.

"Where would a shell get stained with tar in Aventurine?" Kano asked.

"Only one place," the crab said. "Bristolmeir."

9

The Junkyard

My fur stood on end. "Is Bristolmeir nearby?" I asked.

"It's not far," the crab said. "Turn right at the end of the canyon, and go straight until you come to the glitter walk."

I moved as quickly as I could to get down to the lower levels of the shell and then jumped back into the seawater pool and, with renewed energy, shifted into a spiny dart. I didn't even have to look at Kano to do it. The food and rest had totally restored my strength. Bristolmeir was just around the corner!

I was closing in on the fourth and fifth shards of the Yugen Lineage mirror. Only I wasn't in as much of a hurry to complete my mission. Leaving Aventurine meant leaving Kano, and I would miss him.

Kano followed me out of the shell. I could tell he was just as anxious to reach Bristolmeir—he was clearly worried about it. If the tarred shell had come from the underwater city like the hermit crab said, something awful had happened there.

With our streamlined bodies and bristle defenses, we sped through the canyon without any trouble. Except for an occasional curious glance, we passed unnoticed. Even so, when the slope of the canyon wall became flush with the floor, my nerves were frayed.

"That was too easy," I said. "I just know something nasty is waiting for us up ahead."

"Maybe, but at least we'll be going in the right direction," Kano said. "The Bristolmeir compass potion is working again."

"Awesome!" I was honestly thrilled. Having something go right eased the dread, but only slightly. I had been ambushed too many times in Aventurine.

After we turned toward Bristolmeir, the abundance of life dwindled. Within minutes, we were swimming through a dead zone. The eerie stillness was creepy.

"Is it supposed to be like this?" I didn't try to hide the tremor in my voice.

"No," Kano said. "I've never been to Bristolmeir, but I've spoken with many who have. Everyone says it's a paradise of light and joy."

"Maybe it is." I didn't like seeing Kano so upset.

"See for yourself," Kano said sadly. "Look."

The dome of Bristolmeir loomed in the distance. It was so dark, it looked like a black hole in the ocean. No light reflected off or shone through the surface, and an overwhelming sense of foreboding washed over me.

As we drew near, I could see how awful things really were. A thick carpet of black tar and ooze coated the ground. Scattered bits of debris grew into huge piles of junk. Even the water was cloudy.

I knew from Okasan's stories that disasters strike Aventurine just like they do in the waking world. I was about to ask Kano what he thought had befallen Bristolmeir. Then I saw a glimmer of light in the muck.

"A shard!" I shouted and shot forward. But when I got nearer, I could see my mistake. The glint came from sparkling crystals embedded in the ground under the tar.

"We've been swimming along the glitter walk, and we didn't even know it," Kano said.

"Why hasn't someone cleaned this up?" I asked.

"I don't know." Kano's tone shifted between sadness and anger as we continued toward the dome. "Fairies recycle everything. Nothing goes to waste, so there's no junk or trash in Aventurine. At least, there wasn't. Hey, what's that?"

He paused to stare at some glass sitting on a low mound.

At first glance, I thought it was a round lightbulb. I was wrong. "It's a snow globe!"

Kano and I both peered at the tiny crystal towers, domes, and arches depicted in the glass.

"It's Bristolmeir," Kano said. "Exactly like I imagined it would be."

"Really? It's not what I imagined at all." When Queen Kumari had first mentioned a city at the bottom of the sea, I had pictured the ancient buildings, gardens, and mountainous countryside of Japanese mythology. My mother's descriptions had been very vivid.

"Bristolmeir as it was, not as it is." Kano sighed as he turned away.

I looked up and shrieked, "There's the shard!"

"Where?" Kano asked.

"On that old sofa over there." I was so excited, I started swimming before I finished talking.

The sofa was half-buried in a pile of broken beds, old quilts, giant rotting toadstools, and baskets. Shard number four was tangled in a fishnet and stuffed in a jar with a long, thin neck. The jar was wedged between two springs that had popped through the sofa seat. It didn't look like the shard would be difficult to retrieve, but I had to be sure.

"Is there anything here that could hurt me?" I asked Kano.

Kano studied the jar and sofa from several angles. "I don't see anything."

Satisfied that nothing nearby would attack me, I tackled the problem. The mirror wouldn't appear until the shard was free. I tried to pull on the net and pull the shard out of the jar with my teeth, but my long spiny snout didn't fit through the neck. I had to break the jar to reach the shard.

"I need hands to . . ." I turned to look for a heavy tool and froze. While my back was turned, Kano had transformed into the beautiful boy Queen Patchouli had sent to guide me.

Or rather, half of him was a boy.

Below the waist, Kano had a much larger aquatic tail. He had exchanged his gray-green spiny dart scales for sparkling green and gold.

I was so startled and happy that all I could do was sputter and stare. I didn't even start to change.

For a brief moment, Kano's eyes sparkled with mischief. He obviously thought my reaction was hilarious. Instead of the tunic and shirt he'd had on in the cave, he wore an open vest made of polished shells and woven seaweed. His hair fanned out in the water.

When I found my voice, I was still a spiny dart, and I was furious. "Does this mean I could have been a beautiful mermaid all this time?"

Kano shook his head. "A mermaid couldn't have survived all the dangers we encountered. But now, since you need hands, it seemed like a good idea."

"A very good idea!" Changing into a mermaid was easy. My top half quickly became Sumi with gills, and my bottom half copied Kano's tail. I kept the top of my dress, my scarf, and my bracelets from the fairy wardrobe.

"Do I look ridiculous?" I spotted a metal hubcap and swam closer to look for my reflection. I tilted my head back and forth, but the hubcap was too dull to reflect.

"You're just like every mermaid or river maiden I've ever met," Kano said. "They all spend a lot of time preening and staring at their reflections."

I made a face at him and pretended to pout.

Kano grinned back at me, but his smile fled in a flash of alarm. "Get your shard!"

I spun and gasped when I saw a black starfish sliding over the back of the sofa, leaving a trail of yellowish goo.

It was bigger than the hubcap and only inches from the jar. If the starfish stayed on course, the shard would be glued to the sunken couch. I wouldn't be able to free it, and Takara wouldn't appear.

There was no time to waste. I was too frantic to shift into something that could smash the jar, so I yanked the silver scarf off my neck and wrapped the cloth around my hand. Then I gripped the jar and pulled. The scarf protected my hand when the jar's neck broke off, and it saved me from being cut when I reached into the broken glass. When I had the netting and the shard, I launched myself clear with a flip of my powerful new tail.

I tore the netting away from the shard as I swam to Kano's side. Then I called the mirror. "Takara's truth!"

When the mirror appeared, the golden flash blazed like a star in a midnight sky. As the fourth shard snapped into place, more tarnish and grit vanished from the brass frame. I took heart from the brilliance of the talisman in the midst of so much darkness and destruction. It felt like Okasan was letting me know that everyone in the Yugen Lineage was with me.

After the mirror disappeared, I asked Kano, "Can we keep this form?"

"For now," Kano said with a lopsided grin. "I know you like being beautiful."

"That's true, but . . ." There was more to it than that. I wasn't sure I could explain it, but I tried. "Being a mermaid feels better than being a fish. Even this tail seems more natural."

"Maybe because it's a mammalian tail," Kano said.

"That's it!" My eyes lit up. Fish tails move from side to side. My new tail moved up and down like a dolphin's or a whale's. "I'm glad you understand."

"I do," Kano said, "very well."

The black starfish stayed close to the bottom, and nothing else swam in the murky water above the junkyard. With no obstacles or threats to slow us down, we reached the city in good time. As we approached the towering entrance, my gaze was drawn up across the intricate lattice of the dome. Here and there I saw a hint of gleaming metal beneath the black tarnish that was corroding the surface of the structure. It was easy to envision the dome in its glory, and my heart ached for the lost beauty.

Bristolmeir's fate was worse than I had imagined.

"How could this happen?" I asked.

At a loss for words, Kano shrugged and shook his head.

An unexpected, high-pitched screech shattered the silence and brought both of us to a lurching halt.

I didn't have to ask Kano what monster had made the frightening noise. The creature stood between us and the gateway into the city.

The beast was twenty feet tall and covered in overlapping red plates. Its face was a fusion of human and crustacean features with a flat nose, spiny whiskers, and black recessed eyes. It had two sturdy armored legs with spiny hair along the back edges and feet with three clawed toes. Both arms were armored like the legs, with a hook and a clamp instead of hands.

"What is it?" I whispered to Kano.

"I am Krogan, guardian of Bristolmeir gate!" the monster roared.

I had come too far to be stopped by a bellowing lobster. Argo had allowed us to pass when he learned my identity as a fairy-godmother-in-training. I hoped the same thing would work with Krogan. Drawing on every ounce of courage I possessed, I swam in front of Kano to state my case.

"I am Sumi Hara of the Yugen Lineage, and I'm on a mission to find the pieces of my family's lost talisman. The last piece is in Bristolmeir, but you are blocking the way in," I said.

Krogan leaned over to peer into my eyes and softened his voice. "My job is not to keep you out."

I blinked. "Then what are you doing here?"

Krogan straightened and swept his arm across

130

the vista of trash and debris. "I am here for the same reason the Bristolmeir fairies and mermaids built this barrier around the city: to keep the evil Queen Mitsu and her rot in."

I tensed at the mention of an evil queen. Jealous, power-crazed women existed in fairy tales written by old men in the 1800s, but no such beings lived in Aventurine. Okasan would have told me . . . unless she didn't know.

Kano didn't dispute Krogan's claim. He seemed relieved.

"The fairies dumped all this junk, Kano!" I exclaimed. "Why aren't you upset?"

"Because they dumped it for a reason," Kano said. "Anything that serves a useful purpose isn't junk."

"Okay," I agreed. "Imprisoning an evil queen is a good reason to litter, but it's hard to believe someone that horrible lives in Aventurine."

Frowning, Kano flicked his tail in agitation and asked the guardian, "How did someone so evil take over?"

"Queen Mitsu wasn't always evil." Krogan sat on his haunches and sighed. "She was once as beautiful and gentle as all the fairies and creatures of Bristolmeir. She adored gardens and sculptures and mosaics, and she encouraged everyone to use their talents to create beauty."

"What changed?" Kano asked.

"In time, the fairies' creations weren't beautiful enough," Krogan explained. "Queen Mitsu wanted everything to be perfect, and her quest for perfection corrupted everything and everyone within her realm."

I was shocked. "Why hasn't she noticed that her realm has become trashed?"

The giant lobster creature sighed again. "She lives alone beneath Bristolmeir, where her delusions shield her. Anytime she tries to surface, the sight of the junk drives her back down to her shelter. We thought it was safer to contain her in her denial. She's very powerful."

"But it should never have gotten this bad," Kano said. "Fairies always band together to convert evil to good or to drive it out."

"We tried," Krogan growled. "When the darkness and rot first began to creep through the crystal corridors, all the fairies of Bristolmeir sought to reverse the queen's evil influence—and failed."

"Please, forgive my confusion," Kano said, "but I do not understand why all could not stop one."

"She *is* a queen, Kano," I said.

"We waited too long," Krogan added. "Everyone hoped Queen Mitsu would realize that beauty isn't perfect and perfect isn't possible, but she didn't. Then her power suddenly surged, and our chance was lost."

"But you can't give up!" I glared at the creature.

"I haven't," Krogan said, "but all I can do now is prevent the queen's corruption from spreading beyond the realm of Bristolmeir."

I felt bad for him and for Bristolmeir, and despite Krogan's dedication, I feared that the queen's evil might spread to infect all of Aventurine. I wanted to help, but first I had to complete my mission.

"Will you let us enter the city?" I asked.

"Of course," Krogan answered. "But anyone who enters might become tainted as well, and go on to spread evil throughout Aventurine. So you can go in, but you can never come out."

10

Bristolmeir

Krogan's threat scared me. I did *not* want to be trapped forever under the Bristolmeir dome, but I had to enter. The final shard was in the city.

"Are you sure you want to go on?" Krogan asked as Kano and I swam past.

I paused and looked up into the guardian's face. Even with his grotesque features, I could tell he feared for our safety. "Yes, Krogan, I'm sure. I can't abandon my quest. But don't worry. We'll be fine."

"I wish you well," Krogan said, "but nothing within Queen Mitsu's domain is ever fine."

Disturbed but committed, I put the warning out of my mind and joined Kano.

The entrance to Bristolmeir was a solid white gate that stretched forty feet from the ground to the peak of the arch. It was embossed with delicate designs that reminded me of scrimshaw, the sailor's art of black etchings on whalebone. Instead of old ships, whales, and sailing artifacts, the gate was covered with pictures of ocean and land life: anemones, clams, fish, and lacy seaweed were twined with flowers, birds, odd little animals, and fairies with elegant fins instead of wings. But like everything else in the underwater city, the beautiful gate was corroded by the queen's evil. Splotches of black rot and mold were visible on the white surface. Pits and cracks marred the details in the etchings, and the colors in the embossed lines were bleeding together.

"How do we open the gate to get in?" Kano called back to Krogan.

"I'm starting to like you guys," the creature said. "I won't help you on your journey to doom."

I'd never been so annoyed by someone liking me before.

Staring straight at the door didn't reveal any cracks or knobs. Kano ran his hands along the edges to see if that would trip a secret catch to make the door open. In fashion, I know that I always have to look at a dress from different angles to make sure that it fits correctly. I stood off to the side and tried to let my eyes see the door without looking right at it. Suddenly I noticed a large circular dent near the bottom. Measuring four feet across, it was decorated like a sand dollar and divided into five sections.

"Is the dome filled with air?" I asked.

Kano nodded. "Yes, but water breathers live inside, too."

"Then the entrance has to work for both, right?" I pressed the drawing in the middle of the sand dollar design.

The gate slid open and closed behind us after we swam into a large entry pool. The walls were made of the same off-white substance as the gate and showed similar signs of damage. Two channels split off from the pool, one to the right and the other to the left. There was air above us. Even in the gray gloom, I recognized the pattern of light on the surface of the water.

"Mermaids have lungs, too," Kano said. "Our gills will shut down as soon as we leave the water."

"Then let's go!" I said, smiling at him to cover up how nervous I was to be entering this evil queen's lair.

What if the fifth shard was buried in the ruins of her realm, never to be found? What if she discovered us here and decided to punish us?

I pushed the negative thoughts to the back of my mind and leapt out of the water. Although my lungs immediately began to take in air, I needed a moment to adjust. Sitting on the edge of the round pool with my tail dangling in water, I wrung out my hair and studied the large chamber.

It was shaped like an upside-down bowl. The walls were covered with shells of various sizes and shapes.

Several really large snail-like creatures huddled in an alcove on the far wall. At first, I thought they were dead. Then I realized they were just moving really slowly. A few creatures that looked like miniature Krogans slept inside the transparent snail shells. A worn path followed the curve of the wall and gradually descended into the pool.

"Why are those snail shells in here?" I asked in a whisper.

"They were underwater transports before Queen Mitsu made them sick," Kano explained.

"I think we should leave before those little lobster things notice us."

"I think you're right." Kano pulled his tail out of the water. "Would you rather be an animal with a hard shell for protection or something that can run fast and hide?"

"*I* can run fast and hide." I promptly lifted my tail and completed the transformation into Sumi the girl. I was still wearing the clothes from the fairy wardrobe: lace-up sandals, gray-blue dress, silver scarf, and beaded bracelets.

Without comment, Kano changed into a whole boy, dressed in the blue tunic, white shirt, gray leggings, and black boots he'd had on when we first met. His clothes were dry.

My dress and scarf were wet. I shivered, but I didn't tell Kano I was cold. I closed my eyes and pictured water evaporating from the fabric. Thirty seconds later, my clothes were dry, too.

I was feeling really proud about what I'd figured out, but before I could brag, one of the snails squeaked. I glanced over just as a minilobster slid out from under the shell.

"Let's go!" I tugged on Kano's sleeve.

We spotted a larger sand dollar door in the wall just as the creature noticed us. It shrieked and gave chase, waving two of its clawed legs. It slipped on the smooth ground, and we easily beat it to the door, which opened as we approached and closed after we sprang through. I looked at the engravings on the door to figure out if there was a lock, but it seemed like the door had automatically locked itself.

"I wasn't sure about this form, Sumi," Kano said as he gave his arms and legs an approving once-over, "but it might be the best for traveling through the city. It won't be ideal for everything, though," he added. "Luck as much as ability kept the minimonster from catching us. We might have to transform again if our circumstances change."

"I know," I said with a smile. "But if it rains, I won't grow a toadstool on my head."

"Well, I guess a bat-wing umbrella or duck-feather hair will repel water just as well."

"Psh. No, I'm over all of that," I said.

Kano grinned. "Duck-feather hair is too . . . yesterday?" he asked.

"Exactly," I said with a wink.

At the moment, nothing threatened us, and we paused to take stock of our surroundings. The area outside the entrance door had been a plaza with gardens, mosaic pathways, pools, and crystal fountains. The plants had withered and rotted. The paths were riddled with potholes and cracks, and the water in the pools had dried up or stagnated.

Is everything in Bristolmeir festering in Queen Mitsu's evil? I wondered, and glanced back at the door. The sand dollar pattern had been damaged by moldy crud, but the door still operated. And now that I wasn't running for my life, I could spare a moment for simple curiosity.

"Why did the door open for us and not the creature?" I asked Kano.

"Because your goody-good-goodness hasn't been spoiled by Queen Mitsu," a silky voice said. "And that creature was a fairy once. She didn't escape the queen's evil, sad to say."

The speaker was hidden behind a tangle of black thorns and vines. Kano carefully parted the dead foliage.

A brown dog with floppy ears was sprawled

across a large rock. A milky film covered its eyes, and its black nose was dry and cracked. A gray tongue dangled from one side of its mouth. When I looked closer, I realized that the dog had a seal's body and flippers with dog paws. Its curly, coarse brown coat was bare in spots, and tufts of lost fur had been pushed into a pile.

"Why did the creature chase us?" I asked.

"To warn you or to eat you," the dog replied. "It doesn't matter now. You are here, and soon you will be lost, too."

"Who are you?" I asked.

"I am Darcy, the fairy's faithful companion," the dog said. "Now I stand watch, keeping Ilsa safe in the futile hope that the queen will be stopped and Bristolmeir reborn."

Kano pointed to a large black pod in the mud beside the rock. "Is Ilsa in that cocoon?"

"Yes." The dog groaned as it turned to look. "A few fairies managed to hibernate. Others were corrupted. I know not what became of those who left. They were determined to stop Queen Mitsu's horror from spreading."

"They tried and failed, it seems," Kano said.

"And her power is growing." Darcy sighed and began to nod off.

The evil that infected the city felt tangible now.

Besides a sour taste in the air, I could sense a pitch-black darkness seeping through my pores and into my blood. I wanted to run.

But I couldn't.

I had been entrusted with the honor and talisman of my fairy godmother lineage. I couldn't leave until the Yugen mirror and my mission were complete.

Queen Kumari's helpful hint suddenly flashed through my mind: *The last shard lies beneath Bristolmeir, at the bottom of the sea.*

"How do I get under the city?" I asked, but I was too late. The dog had fallen asleep and didn't stir when Kano nudged it. "Everything is such a mess. We'll never find the way."

"Yes, we will," Kano said.

"How can you be sure?" I glanced down the remains of three walkways. "Queen Patchouli's compass potion was only designed to find Bristolmeir, not the shards."

"You found the first four," Kano said, "or they found you."

I hadn't thought about it before, but I realized Kano was right. The missing mirror pieces had always shown up where I was sure to find them. I had no choice now but to follow my instincts and hope they led me to the last one.

"Which way?" Kano asked.

None of the three paths beckoned, so I chose the one in the middle. I didn't have a reason. It just seemed like the right thing to do.

It was obvious that the interior of Bristolmeir was exactly like the tiny replica in the snow globe. Crystal towers connected by intricate arches rose toward the domes. In the snow globe, the prisms had shone with all the colors of the rainbow. Now, the facets, lines, and curves were deformed and lumpy, like plastic cups that had been melted in an oven. Trees of all shapes and sizes stood out like black silhouettes. Every branch was bare, and yellow-brown sap trickled out through rotted bark. A cold, drizzling mist fell from the gray cloud that hovered over the city, and shadows quickly smothered any lingering sparks of light that defied the queen's evil.

As Kano and I walked, being careful not to step on clusters of stinging nettles or black fairy cocoons, Queen Mitsu's quest for perfection troubled me. I had always thought perfection was good, something people wanted to achieve. But now, seeing the twisted version of beauty around me, I realized maybe I'd been wrong. Nothing could be really and truly perfect. Maybe that was the answer: nothing was perfect except nothing. And slowly, given enough time, everything would decay and erode until nothing remained.

Not even Queen Mitsu.

Surely Queen Kumari and Queen Patchouli wouldn't allow another fairy queen to destroy Aventurine.

Unless they didn't realize what was happening.

"Watch it!" Kano pulled me to the side, just before I stepped in a puddle of liquid tar.

"Thanks." I grimaced, then winced with pain. "Ouch!"

"What?" Kano asked in alarm.

"Something pinched me!" I looked down, squealed, and jumped up onto a flat rock. A hundred segmented worms marched past me like an army with a thousand legs. They were eating all the vegetation in their path. "One of them bit me! Does that mean I'll catch the rot?"

"I don't think so," Kano said. "Everything in Bristol-meir has been damaged over time, and we just got here. Still, you need something to protect your feet."

I glanced down at my bare toes. The sandals I had picked out were pretty, but totally wrong for hiking through a broken city that swarmed with nasty creatures.

Keeping a wary eye out for other creepy crawlies, I followed close behind when Kano entered a building.

"This was a fairy's home," Kano said softly.

"It's so sad." A rush of emotion caught in my

throat as I looked around the ruins.

A large tree stood in one rounded corner. The yellow sap seeping through the bark was full of sawdust from wood bores that squirmed in and out of holes in the trunk, eating the tree from the inside out. The crystal roof, which had adapted to fit the tree's slow growth, was stained and cracked by fallen branches. The soft moss carpet had become brittle and had turned to dust under our feet. A cup of sour milk curd and a hardened cake sat on a blackened toadstool table. A gossamer gown, abandoned in the fairy's rush to flee, lay shredded on a grass hammock.

The evil rot, which had started slowly according to Krogan, had quickly overwhelmed Bristolmeir when Queen Mitsu's power surged.

"I think these were boots." Kano held up two lumps of leather. "It's hard to tell."

I rummaged through the clothes hanging on bent hooks in the fairy's closet. The sandals weren't my only wardrobe problem. My dress and scarf were too flimsy to keep me warm and safe. The army of worms had scared me, but something worse could attack my bare arms and legs. If I couldn't find clothes, I'd have to shape-shift protective adaptations, but I'd rather save my energy.

The delicate fabrics in the fairy's gowns were unraveling, but I found gold pants and a red jacket with faded flower appliqués. Ignoring the tears in the knees, I slipped the pants on under my dress. The jacket cloth had worn thin, but the long sleeves covered my arms.

In the next house, I found a floppy gardening hat and a pair of boots that would actually provide some protection from the elements.

Kano used an upside-down basket tied on to his head with frayed twine to keep the rain off. If we hadn't been in the middle of a dying city, I would have laughed. We looked like thrift-store rejects in our rags and makeshift accessories, but with all our bright colors, we were still the height of fashion in Queen Mitsu's Bristolmeir.

I wondered what the queen looked like, then decided it would make no difference. Queen Mitsu could be as elegantly beautiful as a geisha on the outside, but she would still be as ugly as her evil heart.

When Kano asked which way we should go, I pointed toward the center of the city. "It's the logical place to look for a way under the dome."

"What makes you think so?" Kano asked as he pushed pieces of a crushed fountain off the path.

"Intuition," I said with a shrug. Every mall I had ever been to—in Japan and America—had escalators in or near the center.

The farther we went, the harder the conditions

became. Like the tree in the fairy house, the blight had stricken Bristolmeir in the center and was working its way out. Every obstacle made me more grateful for the clothing we had scavenged. As we scrambled over a huge pile of downed trees and broken crystal, I slipped in the loose debris. I slid halfway back down on my stomach, but I wasn't cut or scratched.

At one point, the path and surrounding area had caved in, so we ducked into a tunnel that was just big enough to crawl through.

"Let's hope that whatever dug this tunnel isn't still in it," Kano said as he crawled into the dark.

I had an idea. "Maybe we should turn into something worse than whatever made the tunnel. Just in case we run into it."

Kano craned his neck to look back at me. "Like what?"

"Like this!" I closed my eyes to get a good picture planted in my mind. Then I transformed into an alligator.

"What are we?" Kano asked as he copied my form.

"Alligators," I said. "They are very mean, very fast swamp creatures with big teeth and strong jaws." I couldn't help but feel proud as we barreled through the tunnel on short, sturdy legs. I didn't even mind the mud. I was confident that nothing could bite through my tough hide.

"I have to remember that one," Kano said, after we emerged into daylight and changed back into human form. "There might be alligators in Aventurine, but I've never seen one."

"I never thought I'd like being one." I grinned.

We were near the center of the city. All the flowers and leaves had crumbled or were soggy with rot. Giant toadstools had collapsed under the weight of their caps, and piles of moldy spores had collected under tall brown ferns. Six channels fed into a large central pool, but the water was green and smelled like sewage. Insects, two-headed snakes, and bald rodents flitted, slithered, and scurried over everything.

"Well, aren't you a sight for sore eyes."

Kano and I both snapped our heads in the direction of the gravelly voice. At first glance, I thought a vulture sat on the back of a sagging park bench. But as we cautiously walked closer, I realized that the speaker was a hunchbacked fairy with beady black eyes and a beaked nose. Her toes were curled like talons, and she was wrapped in a tattered black cloak. She looked like a Halloween witch. Was this Queen Mitsu?

"You don't belong here," the witch fairy snapped.

Kano wasn't afraid. "Queen Patchouli sent us."

"Did she now," the fairy scoffed. "And what terrible crime did you commit to warrant such punishment?"

"None," Kano answered.

"I'm on a mission," I said, stepping up.

"In training, are you?" The fairy's harsh tone softened. "What lineage?"

"Yugen," I said. "I have to get below Bristolmeir to finish my quest. Do you know the way?"

"I do," the witch fairy said, "but there's nothing under Bristolmeir except Queen Mitsu's City of Mirrors."

"What?" I gasped. A whole city of mirrors? Finding the fifth mirror shard there would be impossible.

"You should be afraid!" The dark fairy wagged a bony finger in my face. "Go back while you can."

"I have to go on," I said, hoping she didn't notice the tremor in my voice. "Please, show me how to get below."

The witch fairy hesitated, then pointed at the tower in the center of the dome. "The door is in that spire. The lift no longer goes up, but it might still go down." Without another word, she pulled her cloak over her head.

"How am I supposed to find one little piece of mirror in a city of mirrors?" I asked Kano as we headed toward the central tower.

"You'll know it when you see it," Kano said.

I exhaled, still troubled. "It's not just that. I was hoping to avoid Queen Mitsu. I thought I'd see the last shard and we'd escape."

"I was hoping that, too." Kano stopped, took my hand, and smiled. "Don't worry. We'll be okay as long as we stick together."

"You're a great guide, Kano," I said, "but you're an even better friend. Thanks."

"You're welcome, Sumi."

The tower was much bigger than it appeared from a distance. The base was at least sixty feet wide on all six sides. Shadows and black webs haunted crystal facets that had once sparkled with diamond light. Large garden boxes at each corner were overgrown with black thorns and iron vines, and most of the walkway mosaic tiles had been shattered.

"That must be the door," Kano said.

I followed his gaze toward a round sand dollar door in the wall. It looked just like the other doors except it was bigger and totally black. All the creatures digging, flying, and hunting around the tower plaza gave it a wide berth.

Kano and I walked up to the door, but the sections didn't slide open when I pressed the center knob.

"It's stuck," I said.

"Maybe I can pry it open." Kano dashed over to

the nearest garden box and broke a black thorn off the stem. He held it like a knife. "These thorns are as hard as steel."

When the door suddenly opened, I was so excited I hopped in. "C'mon, Kano! We don't need—"

The door slammed closed. I pressed the inside knob over and over, but the door didn't open again.

According to Darcy the dog, the entry door had deliberately closed to keep the minilobster from following us. Now I suspected that Kano and I had been separated on purpose as well. Making the mirror whole was my mission. If I wanted to continue my training as a fairy godmother, I had to complete this last leg on my own.

I was honor-bound to uphold my family's traditions, but I also wanted to succeed for myself— not out of duty or because it was expected. No calling could be more satisfying than designing gorgeous clothes every girl could feel good about wearing.

And I was one step closer to being able to do that—I just had to find the fifth shard.

As I glanced around the lift for a down button, a clear bubble emerged from the walls and encased me. That was when the floor disappeared, and I started to fall.

11

Reflections of Evil

I screamed.

Who wouldn't? I was falling into a bottomless abyss. Luckily, it wasn't actually an abyss or bottomless, and my scream ended as abruptly as the bubble stopped. I sat inside it, hovering a foot off a glass floor, until the bubble burst and dumped me. I landed with a thud and inhaled sharply, but the glass underneath me didn't break.

Shaking and winded from the fall, I paused to catch my breath and get my bearings. A few deep inhales and slow exhales restored my breathing, but I couldn't get oriented. The walls of the chamber were covered with tiny mirrors. In the dim light, thousands of distorted images created a surreal Sumi collage.

I had definitely fallen into Queen Mitsu's City of Mirrors.

I didn't see a way out of the bubble chamber, but there had to be one. I crept forward on my knees and carefully felt along the walls with my hands. There was a break in a corner, obscured by the endlessly reflecting mirrors. One wall stopped short, and the other extended far beyond it. The exit led into a corridor filled with broken mirrors covering the floor, ceiling, and walls.

My heart pounded, sounding like thunder in my ears. I didn't want Queen Mitsu to know I was here, if it wasn't already too late. I might have triggered an alarm when I landed.

I took another deep breath to calm my nerves and crawled along the corridor. The ceiling looked high enough for me to stand, but I was wary of optical illusions. I didn't want to shatter a mirror, either. The glass might cut me, and the sound would surely give away my location. I got to my feet very slowly, feeling the air above me with my hands in case a mirror was closer than I imagined. Once standing, I moved forward as though walking on eggshells.

The corridor ended at a T, with two corridors branching off to each side. I turned left because it felt like the right way to go. At the next three intersections, I made another left, then two rights. A sense of direction wasn't possible in the mirrored maze, and I had to rely on my intuition alone.

Confusion wasn't the only bad effect the mirrors had on me. I had a pounding headache, and then I walked straight into a mirror at the end of a dead-end passage. The tilt of the mirror had made it look like the passage continued on. In the next corridor, I stumbled over a camouflaged step. Then the ceiling suddenly dropped lower, and I bumped my head.

I was getting frustrated. I tried not to think about wandering, lost and aimless, until I collapsed. I just kept walking, trusting that the shard and I would find each other.

Queen Mitsu found me first.

I heard an amused cackle that couldn't have come from anyone else. The evil fairy queen was watching me. The hairs on my skin rose, and my throat went dry.

Her mean laugh echoed through the twisted maze. Apparently, she thought my fumbling progress was highly entertaining, and that annoyed me. I came to a wide hub area where five corridors branched off, and I finally saw myself in a large full mirror. My image wasn't broken up into a hundred parts, and I realized Queen Mitsu had another reason to be amused.

The queen's poison had caught up with me.

My beautiful black hair was a mess of dry bristles, and my face was covered with red warts and pimple scars. As I watched, my white teeth turned black, and my fingernails grew into hooked talons.

"What did you do to me?" My eyes flashed. I didn't need the wicked queen to tell me that I was turning into a monster like the fairies. I just wanted her to know I wasn't afraid. I was angry.

"No need for tantrums, dear," Queen Mitsu cooed, mocking my distress. "Soon you'll be perfect."

"I was perfect before." I began to shift back into my normal form. "Ha!" I exclaimed with triumph when the warts and pimple scars began to fade.

"What a foolish girl," the queen said as the blemishes returned. This time there were black lumps that oozed yellow stuff, too.

I fought her with every ounce of strength I had, but the fairy queen was stronger. She countered each of my successes with something worse. My rotting hair fell out in clumps, and the skin under my fairy rags hardened and cracked.

"You can't win." Queen Mitsu spat out the words with ridicule and contempt. "No one has more power within Bristolmeir and the City of Mirrors than I, especially not a girl who has barely begun her fairy godmother training."

I stopped trying to undo the queen's awful changes, but I wasn't giving up. It was just smarter to conserve my strength. I needed it to retrieve the fifth shard, which was still hidden in the midst of a million other mirrors.

Since nothing was keeping me there, I chose the middle corridor and scanned all the mirror images as I walked. For a while, only pieces of Sumi-the-ugly-and-gross were visible. Then, bits of an unfamiliar figure began to appear, and I started to piece together an image of the fairy queen.

She might have been beautiful once, but not anymore.

In Queen Mitsu's journey toward perfection, she had lost all her hair, muscle mass, and coloring. She looked exactly how I had always pictured a goblin. Wrinkled gray skin clung to a stooped, bony frame. Her black eyes were sunken into a skeleton face, and the nostrils of her flattened nose flared above thin, parched lips. Torn gray fairy wings hung limply from her hunched back.

She was shriveling out of existence, but I suspected she wouldn't disappear until everything else was gone, too.

However, seeing the queen's shrunken condition bolstered my confidence. I didn't have her magical power, but I was physically stronger. That was my only advantage. Queen Mitsu had everything else on her side.

"Who are you?" the queen asked, her voice echoing down the corridors. She was too impatient to wait for my reply. "Where are you from?" she added.

"I am Sumi Hara from Japan." I answered with a partial truth. Queen Mitsu knew I was a young fairy godmother, but judging by her questions, she didn't know my lineage or my mission. I didn't want to give her more information than necessary.

"I do not know this place called Japan," the queen muttered. "Is it in the waking world or a remote part of Aventurine?"

"It's very far away," I said, turning left at the next corridor.

"How did you find my maze?" A lilt of delight brightened the queen's scratchy voice. "Isn't it wonderful?"

"I fell in," I said. "And yes, it's quite amazing."

"There's nothing else like it in all Aventurine," the queen stated proudly.

"That's true," I agreed. Trying to process so many fragmented images was a strain, and I paused to rest my eyes.

"You're much too ugly and imperfect to have been here long," the queen observed. "Did you come seeking my perfection?"

"I got lost." Standing still and with my eyes closed, I could smell something rotting. I was certain the odor came from Queen Mitsu. I wanted to move away from it, but when I opened my eyes, I saw a telltale glint of light.

"Lost and found," the queen said, giggling, "by me."

I didn't respond. The glint could vanish if I looked away even for a second.

"Why have you stopped?" The queen's tone turned sullen. "It's been much too long since I've had company. Hurry up, Sumi Hara from Japan."

"Uh, well . . ." I flinched at hearing my name from her lips, but quickly recovered. "I'm not sure which way to go."

That wasn't a lie. If I moved, I'd lose sight of the shard.

"That's easy!" The queen laughed. "The more mirror images of me you see, the closer you are!"

I had to move or Queen Mitsu would become suspicious. She'd already made me hideous, but at least I was still Sumi. Who knew what she would do if I fought her?

My main goal was getting the final shard. And now I had to risk losing the shard's reflection as I took a step forward to supposedly go find the queen.

The light jumped a dozen mirrors and glinted from a mirror just ahead of my position. When I took another step, the glint jumped forward again. After three more steps, I realized that the glint must have been guiding me to the shard's location in the maze. I tested my theory at the next T. When I turned right, the glint appeared ahead of me. But I didn't see it when I turned and started down the left-side corridor. Now that I was sure the light would keep me on track, I quickened my pace. The sooner I found the shard, the sooner the hand mirror would be whole and my mission would be over.

"What are you doing?" Queen Mitsu asked in an irritated huff.

Flustered, I answered with a question. "What do you mean?"

"You're moving quickly," the queen said. "Are you that anxious to meet me? You're the first to rush to me."

"Of course!" I choked back the lump in my throat and slowed my pace. The queen was so arrogant, I thought she'd believe me. She didn't.

"Or is it that you're looking for something else?" the queen said slyly.

My deception was falling apart. I tried to keep her talking to buy a few more minutes. "I want a piece of the maze as a souvenir." It was a lame excuse, but I couldn't think of any other.

"Then take one," the queen said.

"Thank you, but I want just the right piece. It has to be perfect," I added.

The queen paused. In the silence, I felt like a mouse trapped by a cat that could catch me whenever it wanted.

"I was an ordinary fairy queen once," the queen finally said. "So I'm familiar with all of the fairy godmother lineages, and I know about the Yugen mirror."

I quickened my pace. I was running out of time, but Queen Mitsu seemed to enjoy toying with me. I could only hope that she would leave me with enough time to reach the shard.

"But," the queen continued, "I didn't know that one of the Yugen shards was in my City of Mirrors—until now."

I began to run as quickly as I could without losing sight of the light or ramming into mirrors.

"Queen Patchouli holds on to Takara after the Yugen girls complete their mission," Queen Mitsu said. "Then she scatters the shards for the next Yugen fairy-godmother-in-training to find. This time, I found one first." She hesitated, then exclaimed, "That must be why my power grew so suddenly!"

Why didn't Queen Patchouli take precautions so that the powerful shard wouldn't fall into evil hands? I couldn't think of a reason, unless she didn't know the queen would become evil. Kano hadn't known how bad Bristolmeir had become. Or maybe Queen Patchouli had wanted me to come here and face the queen? That was a scary thought.

"Halt!" the queen screeched.

I didn't obey. I couldn't simply call Takara to claim the fifth shard. It had to be in my possession first.

Queen Mitsu was just as determined to stop me as I was to finish my task. The tiny mirrors lining the corridors suddenly expanded and fused together into large mirrored panels. They reminded me of the distorted mirrors in a horror-movie carnival funhouse. The reflections of my hideous new form were now life-sized in the mirrors surrounding me. The queen's image was much smaller, but it got bigger as she drew closer.

"You can't have the shard back," Queen Mitsu hissed.

Although I could tell she was getting closer, I couldn't pinpoint her location. She, on the other hand, knew exactly where I was in the maze. That put me at an even greater disadvantage.

"It's mine now," the queen growled.

The glint shimmered, as though urging me to move.

I limped down the corridor on newly clawed feet

and two legs that were no longer the same length. I had stopped caring what I looked like, only how the changes affected my ability to survive.

As I approached the next corridor, I suddenly hung back. Queen Mitsu could be waiting just out of sight.

"Boo!" She cackled at her own joke.

I jumped.

The light glided across the face of the large mirror, paused at the edge, and then zipped around the corner.

I fought back my fear and moved ahead, holding my breath until I saw that the connecting corridor was clear. So was the next one. The vastness of the City of Mirrors was helping me, but sooner or later Queen Mitsu would catch up.

That thought stopped me in my tracks. I glanced back, suddenly realizing that Queen Mitsu could just as easily sneak up from behind as ambush me from ahead. There was nowhere to hide in this maze.

Unless she couldn't see me!

As I concentrated on making myself disappear, I thought about Kano. He would love a form that didn't stand out at all.

It was a great idea, but it didn't work. My see-through talons slowly faded, then snapped right back to full visibility again. Becoming transparent took too much energy.

"I told you no one has more power than me." The queen stepped out of a side corridor to stand in front of me. She grinned, amused by my shock.

I couldn't help it—I ran back and ducked into another corridor. It was a useless attempt to escape, and the queen didn't even bother to hurry after me. She could find me anywhere, and there was no need to rush.

As I stood there, unable to decide which way to run, I suddenly had an idea. Maybe there *was* a way to be invisible! I quickly transformed into a copy of the evil queen.

"What?" Queen Mitsu squawked. "Where did you go?"

I froze, hardly daring to hope.

Minutes passed. My image didn't change. From every angle I looked like a mirror image of the queen. I stifled a grin.

"You can't trick me!" the queen raged.

Apparently, I could.

When I caught sight of the glint, I hesitated. The queen was watching the mirrors, trying to get a fix on my position. The instant I started after the light, she would know which image was mine.

I took off.

Part Three
Sewing It Up

12

Takara's Truth

"Got you!" Queen Mitsu snarled as she ran after me.

She was faster and more agile than I would have thought, but I still had the advantage. Queen Mitsu had to pause to sort out our images, while I had the glint to guide me through the maze.

When the glint stopped on a small piece of glass, there was no doubt I had found the fifth missing shard. The glass was wedged into a corner, sparkling like sunlight between gray clouds. I reached up with twisted talons and pulled it free.

"Takara's truth." I spoke the phrase in the queen's gravelly voice, but the family talisman knew it was me. In a flash of golden light, Takara appeared in my hand and the shard snapped right into place.

"No!" Queen Mitsu screamed behind me.

I turned and stared into the fairy's terrified black eyes as the City of Mirrors began to collapse. I clutched the Yugen mirror to my chest. Then I shouted the magic phrase, and the mirror disappeared.

Now I had to worry about me! I had half hoped I would disappear with the mirror and be whisked home again, but no such luck.

Queen Mitsu's black eyes bore into me with hatred. She crouched, ready to spring, when shattered glass rained down on her, momentarily distracting her. The queen ducked and turned to escape, but a large sheet of mirror dropped down to block her escape.

"Help me!" The queen reached out a hand as the walls began to close around her.

She sounded so pathetic, I couldn't ignore her plea. I took a step toward her, but another panel slammed down between us, cutting me off.

The second after the evil queen was trapped, a warm tingling flooded my body. I looked at my arm and gasped as gray leathery skin softened and the muscle fleshed out. I ran my hand through the silken strands of my real hair. I was changing back to Sumi!

But I didn't want to be human. Not yet.

When Takara took the final Yugen shard from the maze, the fairy queen's power must have been suddenly drained. There was no way she could keep the maze of mirrors intact. All around us glass exploded and crashed as the maze broke down. But since Queen Mitsu had been holding the City of Mirrors together, all those pieces were attracted to her like metal shavings to a magnet.

And I was in the way.

A human girl couldn't survive the tons of broken glass streaming toward the powerless queen. I quickly thought of an animal with plates of armor and found myself turning into an armadillo. Now low to the ground, I scrambled away from the tornado of glass surrounding the queen.

My stubby little legs were fast, but my hard claws couldn't dig into the ground. When the force of speeding glass pellets and pieces knocked me off my feet, I curled into a ball. Broken mirrors battered and rolled me about, but the sharp edges didn't penetrate my armored plates.

Queen Mitsu's screams rose above the sounds of glass smashing against glass. She commanded the mirrors to retreat. When they didn't obey, she screeched with rage and then cried out in despair. Before long, a thick wall of glass muffled her sobs.

When all was quiet, I slowly uncurled and looked around.

Every speck of glass in the mirror maze had fused to form a huge sphere that imprisoned Queen Mitsu.

I felt sorry for her, but, in a strange way, encased in a perfectly round, dazzling ball of mirror, she had finally achieved the perfection she wanted.

And I had completed my mission. I had found the five missing pieces of the Yugen mirror *and* defeated an evil fairy queen. That was a totally unexpected bonus. I hoped it meant that Bristolmeir would be restored. I wouldn't know until I found my way back up into the city.

With the mirrors removed, I could see that salmon-colored shells formed the foundation of the city. The shells weren't decayed or littered with debris. They looked bright and new, with gleaming, curved walls.

Since I couldn't sense anything dangerous, I changed back into Sumi and inhaled deeply, savoring a salty breeze. There were no mirrors left to look into, so I patted my hair and face to make sure everything was in the right place. My original fairy dress, scarf, bracelets, and sandals were back on and felt newly washed. I felt as clean and fresh as I had at the beginning of my journey.

After a quick survey, I found a little brook weaving its way through the shells. I followed the flow of the water, hoping it would take me toward the city and not away from it.

In case there were more obstacles to overcome, I resisted an urge to call the brass hand mirror back.

After all I had been through to put it together, I didn't want the mirror to break until Queen Patchouli scattered the pieces for my daughter many years from now.

My daughter?

I was much too young to think about getting married! I didn't even have a boyfriend. I adored Kano in all his strange forms, but he lived in Aventurine. Long-distance friendships could last. Long-distance romances usually did not.

I put these thoughts aside and watched the creatures under Bristolmeir awaken. Like the fairy hiding in a cocoon above, the animals under the city had escaped the queen by hibernating. All sorts of animals, some that I recognized and some that were completely foreign, came out of their nests, caves, and tunnels and looked around as if in a daze. I was trying to find the bubble lift that I had taken down into the City of Mirrors, and I would have completely missed it if a turtle hadn't walked into it. A large bubble popped out of the tube walls and shrunk to turtle size around the passenger. I watched the turtle bubble rise, then rushed forward. It would get me back into the dome.

When a large white bird flew past me and up through the tube, I stopped short and blinked. Apparently, there were two ways back into Bristolmeir: ride the bubble or fly. That was no contest. Transforming into a white bird, I spread my wings.

The sensation of swooping upward through the tube was as thrilling as I had imagined and a thousand times better than flying in my dreams. The wind rushed past, and my wings were in complete control. It was awesome!

I didn't land on the nearest tree when I cleared the hole in the floor. Although tiny hints of green and red leaf buds dotted the branches, the bark wasn't completely healed and sap still oozed out. I couldn't resist flying a few loops around the central tower.

Above me, more and more crystal lights twinkled on until they lit up everything under the dome. The drizzle stopped. Below, the shadows retreated as crushed mosaic walkways became whole and melted towers regained their former shapes.

Wings outstretched, I caught an air current and circled a large plaza garden. Black cocoons vanished in a puff of dust and sleeping fairies stepped out. Dressed in all the colors of the rainbow, they flew on gorgeous wings or danced along the mosaic paths. The underwater city was healing itself and coming back to life.

I had never felt freer or more beautiful in my life, and I almost wished I could stay a white bird that lived in Aventurine.

As usual, Kano brought me back down to earth.

"Having fun?" another white bird asked in Kano's voice.

"Yes!" I laughed, happy to see him. "But I earned it. The City of Mirrors was awful!"

"You found the missing shard," Kano said matter-of-factly.

"It was in Queen Mitsu's mirror maze," I said. "That's why she had so much power."

"Not anymore," Kano said as we flew in a few more lazy circles around the tower. After a moment, he broke away. "C'mon! There's someone you have to meet."

I didn't want to stop flying so soon, but I was anxious to get home. Following Kano, I glided downward into a wooded glade and landed on a large yellow toadstool. I turned back into a girl, and hopped down to the ground.

Kano, the handsome boy with the mischievous smile, landed gracefully beside me.

"Sumi Hara, this is Queen Patchouli of the Willowood Fairies," Kano said.

A tall, regal fairy stepped out from under the toadstool's shadow. She wore a soft green gown with rich golden embroidery. Her hair fell in chestnut waves to her knees, and bees buzzed lazily around her crown of flowers. Her gentle smile and bright

eyes warmed me like a summer sun. The silver-clad
Queen Kumari stepped out to stand beside her.

"It's an honor to meet you, Queen Patchouli." I
spoke softly and bowed.

"And for me to meet you," Queen Patchouli said.
"You restored the Yugen mirror *and* Bristolmeir."

"Your name will be honored in all of Aventurine,"
said Queen Kumari.

Queen Patchouli nodded. "You have
accomplished an extraordinary task
under very difficult circumstances,
Sumi."

"To be honest, I'll kind of miss
all the excitement," I said.

"You'll have plenty of excitement as a fairy godmother," Queen
Patchouli said. "But that's for
another day. Now it's time to call the
Yugen mirror."

My happiness dimmed a little.
Takara wouldn't remain with me. It stayed
with Queen Patchouli in Aventurine. I didn't want to
give it up, but I had to honor the tradition.

"Takara's truth!" The mirror flashed into my hand.

"Look into the glass," Queen Patchouli said.

I hesitated, remembering when I had looked into
the empty frame when I first arrived in Aventurine. I

had seen Kano's image but not my own. What if I still didn't have a reflection?

"Go on," Kano gently urged me.

I raised the glass.

"There's a lot more to Sumi Hara now," Kano said, peering over my shoulder.

My face smiled back at me from the glass. "Why am I glowing?" I asked. My head was ringed by a glowing mist.

"The Yugen mirror sees who we truly are," Queen Patchouli explained. "The aura is the reflection of the warm, caring, and courageous person you are within."

I blushed.

Queen Patchouli smiled and held out her hands.

The box I had found in the antique store appeared. The wood, hinges, and clasp were clean and polished. I could see every detail in the bird, flower, and leaf design.

"I will keep Takara safe until it is next needed," Queen Patchouli said, opening the box. "You can stay in Bristolmeir a while longer, to say your good-byes."

I gently placed the mirror on the silk padding and blinked back tears. With a nod, both queens vanished.

"I'll be sad to see you go," Kano said as we walked through the wooded garden.

"I thought you didn't like me," I teased him to lighten the mood. All around us, fairies and their companions were celebrating.

"Maybe not at first," Kano admitted, "but I do now. That's why I asked Queen Patchouli if I could help with your training."

"Really?" I was so happy, I completely forgot to be coy. I squealed and gave him a huge hug. Then I jumped back. "What did she say?"

Kano laughed. "She said yes."

"She did!" I couldn't stop smiling. "When? Will it be long? Will I still be a shape-shifter?"

"I don't know when," Kano said, "but you *are* a shape-shifter. Now and forever."

Everything was turning out much better than I'd expected. Now that I wasn't saying good-bye to Kano forever, I could enjoy strolling through Bristolmeir with him.

A cluster of yellow bugs with bright red spotted wings flew from flower to flower collecting nectar. Fish jumped and splashed in fountain pools, and birds sang from high perches in trees bursting with new leaves. Fairies danced and laughed as they watered indoor plants and opened windows to let the light into rebuilt homes.

With the walkways fixed and the debris removed, it took us less time to get back to the entrance.

"I want to say good-bye to Krogan," I told Kano.

"I'm not sure you can," Kano said as he led me down a path toward the dome wall.

"Why not?" I asked.

"Because his job is done, and Krogan is the type to only appear when he's needed," a velvety voice said.

"Darcy?" I glanced around the colorful toadstools and flower bushes crowded together in the glen. I didn't spot the dog until she waddled out of the bushes.

"I am happy to see you again," the dog said. Her eyes were clear and bright, and her silky brown fur shone. "Everything is gloriously imperfect again!"

"I'm happy to see you, too. Is Ilsa okay?" I asked.

"She is helping clean up the big mess," Darcy said.

I frowned, puzzled. Since flying into the dome, I had seen crystal buildings, walkways, and other structures rebuild themselves. All the plants, animals, and fairies had recovered from the black rot. The other debris had vanished in puffs of dust like the cocoons or dissolved into the ground.

"What big mess is left?" I asked.

"The one Krogan built to keep Queen Mitsu's evil in," Darcy explained. "That trash won't go away by itself."

"Look." Kano parted a curtain of soft green vines so I could see through the clear dome.

I gasped.

The sea outside Bristolmeir had been transformed from a dark junkyard guarded by a grotesque monster into a bustling paradise filled with fish, fairies, mermaids, and lush fields of seaweed. The water was clear and tinged with a tropical blue-green cast, and the glitter walk sparkled like millions of sequins.

The piles of junk were the only ugly thing left on the picturesque seascape. Fairies and other creatures worked together, moving everything into a large ring that circled the city.

"There must be a way to get rid of the trash," I said.

"It's not trash now," Kano said. "It's a new reef."

I pressed my face against the crystal wall. All along the mound of old, discarded stuff, plants sprouted and colorful buds grew into sea anemones with waving tendrils.

Okasan would love this, I thought with a smile.

"Can we go back out into the water?" I asked Kano.

"The door is right over there," Kano said.

I turned to Darcy. "Good-bye, Darcy. I'm glad we met."

The dog nuzzled my palm. "Farewell, young fairy godmother."

Kano was waiting for me by the sand dollar door.

"Let's be mermaids again!" I exclaimed as the door opened.

"Someday," Kano said, looking sad.

I didn't understand what he meant until I stepped through the door. . . .

I sat up with a start. It was dark, but there was no mistaking where I was. I was back in New York. My green digital alarm clock read 7:21 a.m. My sheets were cool and soft to the touch, and I was wearing my pajamas.

Although I was glad to be home, I felt a twinge of regret for the new friends I had left in Aventurine. I didn't know when I'd see Kano again. I had to be satisfied just knowing I would. In the meantime, there were other friends I had left behind and neglected.

Through the window, I saw that dawn was just beginning to lighten the sky. I turned on my bedside lamp, rushed to my desk, turned on my computer, and opened a blank email. It was evening in Japan.

Hisako!
I am soooo sorry I couldn't talk at lunch. I fell asleep.
Are you there now? Can you set up a chat with Eiko?
Sumi

I tapped my foot, hoping Hisako didn't take too

long to answer. Two minutes later, she sent me a link to a private chat room.

HISAKO: Sumi! I'm so glad to hear from you!

EIKO: Do you like New York? Are American boys cute? Did you get any new clothes?

SUMI: I love New York! It's different than Kyoto, but very exciting. I haven't met any boys yet. :(

I couldn't tell them about Aventurine or Kano or the fairy wardrobe, but that was okay. I didn't want to talk about me. I wanted to know everything that was happening to them.

SUMI: Tell me about Akiyo. Is he as fabulous as Hisako says?

EIKO: OMG! Akiyo is totally in love with her!

HISAKO: ::blushing!:: I am soooooo happy!

SUMI: I am soooooo jealous! ;)

We chatted for an hour, and before we signed off

we set a time to talk again. Then I set my computer and my phone to remind me. Next time I'd have some good stuff I could talk about. School started tomorrow.

I had heard Okasan walk down the hall a bit ago. She always made a traditional Japanese breakfast to get us up early on Sunday, and I was famished!

My room was now flooded with morning light. Although I still loved my pink, yellow, and green color scheme, I thought it might be fun to add some sea-life accents. Curtains and a throw pillow would be easy to find. As I stood up to leave, I glanced at my dresser.

"What?" I exclaimed.

The Bristolmeir snow globe was sitting beside my picture of Hisako, Eiko, and me. I picked up the globe, shook it, and smiled as glitter snow fell around the tiny towers. I didn't know if Kano or one of the queens had saved it for me. I was just thrilled to have it. "Thank you!" I said, in case any lingering magic could hear.

I was so anxious to show the Aventurine artifact to my mother, I didn't stop in the bathroom to comb my hair or brush my teeth. I raced into the kitchen.

"Look, Okasan!" I shook the snow globe in her face.

"It's beautiful!" Okasan set down her wooden

spoon and took the snow globe from my hands. She turned it over to make the snow fall, then frowned. "The bottom is chipped."

I shrugged. "I don't care. I love it!"

"You do?" Okasan's eyes widened with surprise. "Where did you get it?"

"I think Queen Patchouli sent it." I put the snow globe on the center counter. "Or maybe Kano. I don't know."

A slow smile brightened Okasan's face. "Did you go to Aventurine?"

I smiled back and nodded. "Last night. I fixed the Yugen mirror, stopped an evil queen, and saved a whole city!"

My mother gasped. "An evil queen in the fairy world? Now that's a story I want to hear!"

"Can I tell it while we eat?" I asked. "I'm starved!"

"This is such a special occasion, I'm glad I made your favorite breakfast," Okasan said.

"As long as it isn't fuzzy blue fungus or eel eggs, I'll be happy!" I made a face.

Okasan gave me a confused look and set a tray on the counter in front of me. There were bowls of hot boiled rice and miso soup, toasted seaweed with steamed vegetables, grilled fish, and an omelet roll. She handed me a soup spoon and chopsticks and sat down.

"So you met Queen Patchouli," Okasan said.

"Yes, at the end. I didn't start out with the Willo-wood Fairies," I explained. "I was in a cave with Queen Kumari, and she gave me Queen Patchouli's gifts."

"What did you get?" Okasan asked.

"Magic words, a cake, and a boy."

"A boy!" my mother exclaimed. "How did you get so lucky?"

I shrugged. "Kano is a shape-shifter, so he was sent to teach me how to shape-shift."

Okasan nodded. "Did you like it?"

"I loved it! Especially being a mermaid and a bird," I said. "Being an octopus wasn't so great, but it saved me from being Sumi sushi."

Okasan dropped her soup spoon. "Something almost ate you?"

"A big fish, but I turned into an octopus and got away." I paused, then asked, "Kano said that I *am* a shape-shifter. Did he mean in this world, too?"

"Sort of," Okasan said.

"So I can change into a toad?"

Okasan blinked. "Do you want to be a toad?"

"No!" I laughed.

"Good, because you won't be able to change physical forms," Okasan explained. "But you'll be better at the shifting abilities our lineage has always had."

"Like what?" I asked.

"Your grandmother developed the talent of young artists and helped shape their careers," Okasan said. "I find and restore lost treasures and antiquities, which shapes other people's perceptions of history and the world."

"So in a way, changing clothes does count!" I exclaimed.

"Yes," Okasan said. "Creating a fashionable look and designing clothes definitely counts. You'll just be better at it than you were before. Your awakened awareness of others will affect your sense of beauty and improve your style."

I was disappointed that I couldn't change shape in the waking world, but I guess that would have been too good to be true. At least it would help me with my career as a fashion designer.

"So tell me about this evil queen," Okasan said.

"Queen Mitsu wasn't always evil," I explained. "She wanted everything to be perfect, but there's no such thing, so everything around her started turning rotten. She lost her power when Takara claimed the fifth shard."

Okasan clasped my hand. "I'm glad you completed your mission, Sumi."

"Me too." I sighed, a little sadly. "But I wish we could keep the mirror." The snow globe was a nice souvenir, but it wasn't the Yugen lineage talisman. It didn't seem fair that others could keep their family artifacts —

My chopsticks fell from my fingers as I jumped up and touched my face.

"What's wrong?" Okasan asked, alarmed.

"The crescent scar!" I exclaimed. "I completed the mission, but when I looked in the Yugen mirror, the mark wasn't on my face!"

"Takara doesn't reflect what's on the surface," Okasan said.

"Is it . . ." I didn't wait for my mother to answer. I raced through the living room to the bathroom and looked in the mirror. A soft cry escaped me when I saw the half-moon scar on my cheek.

"Are you upset?" Okasan asked softly from the doorway.

"No way!" I grinned. "The mark proves I completed my first fairy godmother mission. You and I are the only two people in the whole world right now who can say that, right?"

Okasan nodded. "Right."

I had been looking forward to entering the Girls' International School of Manhattan for weeks following my trip to Aventurine, but now I was a little worried. For one thing, I wasn't sure how to explain the perfect crescent scar on my face—if anyone was rude enough to ask. Okasan had the same problem when she was thirteen, and she gave me some great advice: tell the truth. The crescent was a family mark, sort of like a birthmark but not exactly.

Then I couldn't decide what to wear. The shocking pink sweater, black skirt, black tights, and ankle boots I had chosen before I went to Aventurine seemed a bit too much for a first day now. I didn't want to stand out for the wrong reasons, and I didn't want to blend in, either. I wasn't a small fish trying not to be lunch for a big fish now. I was the new girl, and I had to wear something that established my identity as a fashionable trendsetter without being too outrageous.

I finally chose my favorite skinny jeans that I'd carefully distressed earlier that year and a deliciously soft V-necked graphic tee that I'd found at the mall with Okasan. It was a gorgeous emerald color and had a design of a white bird pressed onto the front and a white feather centered at the nape of my neck on the back. I pulled my hair into a messy bun so that it wouldn't hide the feather detail, and then laced up my new silver sandals. The white bird and lace-up sandals were straight out of my recent adventures, like an inside joke that only I got. As the final touch,

I slipped on a large, formal cocktail ring that clashed with my laid-back jeans look, but totally worked because it was my only piece of jewelry.

My mother and I took a taxi Monday morning. I got out in front of the school, and Okasan continued on to a meeting at the Asia Society Museum. As I spun around to run inside, I bumped into a boy. He dropped his backpack.

"Watch it, Sawyer!" A girl standing at the top of the steps laughed and shook her head.

The boy and I both ignored her and stooped to pick up the pens and pencils rolling out of the backpack.

"Are you okay?" Sawyer asked.

"I'm fine," I said. "Sorry I ran into you. It's my first day—I wasn't really watching where I was going."

"Um, it wasn't entirely your fault. I sort of . . . well, I sort of deliberately stepped in front of you," Sawyer confessed with a shy smile.

"What?" I asked, mystified.

"When I saw you get out of the cab, I wanted to meet you." Sawyer shrugged. "Somehow, saying 'Hello, my name is Sawyer, I think you're gorgeous' didn't seem dramatic enough."

"I would have remembered that, though," I said, smiling.

"You mean you won't remember this?" Sawyer asked, faking a sad face.

I laughed, and Sawyer relaxed. He had kind eyes, a warm smile, and a sense of humor. If everyone I met in New York was as nice, I was going to love my new life.

Sawyer stood up and slung one strap of his backpack onto his shoulder. He walked backward as he left so he could keep talking. "I go to the boys' school down the block."

"So maybe I'll see you again?" I asked.

"I hope so," said Sawyer.

I watched until he turned and jogged away. Then I took a deep breath and started up the stone steps. The girl who had teased Sawyer was still there, waiting for me.

"Hey, I'm Cameron. My brother is impossible. He thinks he's smooth, but with those big ears, he can't really pull it off," she said.

"I didn't notice his ears," I said. "But all boys are impossible!"

"That is so true!" She sighed.

I followed Cameron into the school. A week ago, I might have been nervous. But after the adventure I'd just been through, I knew that my first day would be a piece of cake.

A Little Piece of Sky

I dove off the edge of sleep
Into the arms of a circus king
He was there
To understand me
Explain the takeoffs
And harder landings

In my dreams I fly
I'm the girl
Who gets the guy
I could bring you a souvenir
Next time
A little piece of sky

Put it in your wishing box
Take it out when you're sad or lost
Take it out and hang with it awhile
Guaranteed to make you smile

In my dreams I fly
I'm the girl
Who gets the guy
I could bring you a souvenir
Next time
A little piece of sky
A little piece of sky

Promise me
A love that lasts forever
And if you can't
Then just
Promise me
A dream

Acknowledgments

Finding and holding a sense of my own beauty has been a lifelong struggle—as I am sure it is for many girls and women. The pictures we see in magazines and of ourselves often don't match reality. What if there were a magic mirror that only reflected how we feel inside? Would we strive to feel good about ourselves instead of looking good for others? Thanks to my family and friends, who are my "magic mirrors." They reflect back the love I give. I shape-shift over time and come out shining with each metamorphosis. Thanks to my friends for sticking by me while I realize my dreams as well as during the times when I don't realize them. Thanks to Lurleen, Dee, Meredith, Jesyca, and Sherry for being there. And finally to Tim, who taught me how to love myself no matter what shape I am in.

About the Author

Jan Bozarth was raised in an international family in Texas in the sixties, the daughter of a Cuban mother and a Welsh father. She danced in a ballet company at eleven, started a dream journal at thirteen, joined a surf club at sixteen, studied flower essences at eighteen, and went on to study music, art, and poetry in college. As a girl, she dreamed of a life that would weave these different interests together. Her dream came true when she grew up and had a big family and a music and writing career. Jan is now a grandmother and writes stories and songs for young people. She often works with her own grown-up children, who are musicians and artists in Austin, Texas. (Sometimes Jan is even the fairy godmother who encourages them to believe in their dreams!) Jan credits her own mother, Dora, with handing down her wisdom: Dream big and never give up.

Trinity's Book

Coming soon!

Meet Trinity—she's always daring herself to climb to new heights, but her trip to Aventurine might just push her over the edge.

Have you read the first
Fairy Godmother Academy book?

*Birdie's
Book*

Will Kerka learn the right Kalis moves
in time to save her sisters?
Find out in

Kerka's
Book

Will Zally's ability to talk with animals
be enough to save a fairy queen?
Find out in

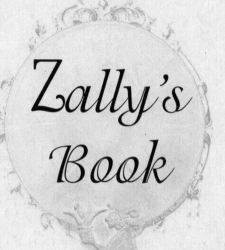

Zally's
Book

Will Lilu's talent for weaving the elements
be enough to stop a magical hurricane?
Find out in

*Lilu's
Book*

Can't get enough of
the Fairy Godmother Academy?

Check out the website for music, games, and more!
FairyGodmotherAcademy.com

The Fairy Godmother Academy is on Facebook!
Become a fan and get all of the latest news
and updates.